SUPER SUNDAYS

SUPER SUNDAYS

by

Ken Rappoport

tempo books

GROSSET & DUNLAP
A Filmways Company
Publishers • New York

SUPER SUNDAYS

Cover photos by Mitchell B. Reibel for FOCUS ON SPORTS

Copyright © 1980 by Ken Rappoport
All Rights Reserved
ISBN: 0-448-17192-9
A Tempo Books Original
Tempo Books is registered in the U.S. Patent Office
Printed in the United States of America
Published simultaneously in Canada

TABLE OF CONTENTS

STEVE BARTKOWSKI

Steve Bartkowski is one of the few players in this book to pick a losing game as his most memorable. But to understand that, you have to understand the California-Stanford football rivalry.

Known as "Harvard-Yale West" in intellectual circles, it is usually among the most civilized of games, almost always pervaded by good sportsmanship and fair play. In short, the best and brightest that college football has to offer.

Conducted on the highest of planes, it is not so much the winning that counts, but more often the effort and the artistry.

"It's the kind of a game you come away feeling good about, win or lose," Bartkowski says.

The so-called "Big Game" of 1974 was one where Bartkowski came away a loser on the scoreboard but a winner in his mind, after his California team was beaten in the final seconds by Stanford.

"It was probably the best game I've ever been involved in," says Bartkowski, now the quarterback for the Atlanta Falcons. "Stanford beat us 22–20 on a 50-yard field goal with three seconds remaining. It was a thrill for me to be involved in that kind of a game. And it seems like those kind of games are played by Stanford and California right down to the wire every year."

It only seems that way because it's so. In more than 80 games, almost half have been decided by a touchdown or less, and there have been ten ties in this remarkably close series. Exemplary of the spirit, excitement, and tradition of college football, the "Big Game" has always meant a big crowd, as there was on this particular day in Berkeley in 1974, Bartkowski's last game for the Golden Bears.

"It was just a great day for football," Bartkowski remembers. "The weather was beautiful; there were 80-some thousand fans in the stands [actually 71,866], and both teams were exciting to watch. We both threw the ball a lot."

Bartkowski threw the ball as much as anyone in the country that season, completing 182 passes in 325 attempts for 2,580 yards and 12 touchdowns, exceptionally high figures by college standards. Stanford featured two fine quarterbacks in Mike Cordova and Guy Benjamin, and everyone came out throwing, as usual. In a list of "Big Game" highlights, the Stanford press guide points out: "Many feel that this Big Game was the most exciting ever."

"They were two high-powered offenses whose emotions were really charged up," says Bartkowski. "It was one of those fun games where the offenses moved up and down the field. They didn't score as many points as the offensive stats would indicate, but the teams did move the football."

Bartkowski completed 20 of 41 passes for 318 yards this day. He threw one touchdown pass and set up a field goal with another good toss. Stanford's two quarterbacks went to the air 31 times during the pass-happy game and completed 12 passes for 222 yards, many of them coming in the frantic fourth quarter in completions by Benjamin.

This was a game that truly saved the best for last. The

Bears had taken a 7–3 halftime lead, courtesy of an 89-yard, 10-play touchdown drive capped by Chuck Muncie's one-yard run in the first quarter. An ineffective Cordova, meanwhile, could only manage to squeeze a second-quarter field goal out of his Stanford team, a 29-yarder by Mike Langford. In the third period, the only scoring was a 34-yard field goal by California's Jim Breech, giving the Golden Bears a tenuous 10–3 lead going into the last period.

Benjamin, who had replaced Cordova late in the third quarter, got Stanford moving with an 11-play drive that resulted in a Langford field goal with just 49 seconds gone in the final period. The defense got the ball back for Stanford, and less than three minutes later the Cardinals scored a touchdown on a one-yard run by Scott Laidlaw for a 13–10 lead.

After intercepting a Bartkowski pass on California's next possession, Stanford turned out the quickest touchdown play imaginable. It took one play, a 60-yard touchdown pass by Benjamin to Tony Hill, to give the Cardinals a 19–10 lead with 7:36 left in the game.

Bartkowski's 35-yard pass to Steve Rivera set up a California field goal with 4:40 to go, cutting Stanford's lead to 19–13. Then, with only 26 seconds remaining, California's All-American quarterback threw a 13-yard TD pass to Rivera for what appeared to be the winning touchdown. The extra point put the Golden Bears into the lead at 20–19, and it seemed unlikely that the Cardinals could come back in so short a period.

But Benjamin made efficient use of what little time he had left, passing to tight ends Ted Pappas and Brad Williams for 18- and 25-yard gains to set up a 50-yard field goal try by Langford.

It seemed an impossible mission to Bartkowski.

"I said there was just no way he was going to make it. They couldn't take this one away from us; this was going to be our day."

But Langford kicked the ball through the uprights, half a football field away, to provide Stanford with a pulsating victory.

"When he kicked it," Bartkowski remembers, "he hit it real good, but one of our guys almost blocked it. He just missed getting a hand on the ball. It happened right in front of our bench. But the ball went through, and when something like that happens, you say to yourself, what else can you do? It's just one of those things."

Langford was a local celebrity after that, Bartkowski remembers. Not only did he win everlasting fame in Stanford football lore, but he was asked to serve as a Santa Claus in the Stanford shopping center.

"I guess I remember that game because it had everything in it," says Bartkowski. "There were great catches, there were long runs. . . . Steve Rivera was our wide receiver and he made some super catches in that game. He made a one-hand grab that was just unbelievable. There's a photograph of it up in the Cal athletic offices now. It was just a beautiful catch . . . he was all stretched out. Everything went according to the way we thought it would. Of course the final score didn't come out the way we planned, but sometimes you just don't really have control over that. The other team was up to the challenge and hit the long field goal to beat us. It was just a real exciting game for me. Sometimes it's not really whether you win or lose in college, it's how well you played. And it just seems that everything jelled for us on that particular day. It was just two teams with their emotions running high, and it was just a matter of a point or two one way or the other. I don't think anybody really lost that day."

Since playing in the pros, Bartkowski has yet to see rivalries that equal the spirit and intensity of Stanford-Cal.

"There are regional rivalries in the pros," he says. "Like, our natural rival would be New Orleans. But in college, it's different, it's stronger. It's a yearly thing, one big game that everybody points to. Coaches' jobs are often won and lost on that particular game, no matter how the season goes for them. The Stanford game for us is just a very, very important game; the emotions run very high, the student bodies back the teams, and it's just great pageantry. It's what college football is all about."

The schools are also on the same competitive level academically, each having produced its share of Nobel Prize winners and professional giants.

"In that rivalry, especially, I think you're dealing with students first and athletes second," Bartkowski says. "And I think you're dealing with a little bit higher IQ oftentimes. Naturally, there were a few players who weren't like that, but overall I think the players that I was associated with at California came from pretty good backgrounds and were pretty intelligent guys, and were there basically to get an education."

Bartkowski's enormous football skills, however, were not overlooked by the Atlanta Falcons, who drafted him in the first round in 1975. Although he did win some Rookie of the Year awards in the National Football League, his first three seasons were generally hampered by injury. Not until his first injury-free season, in 1978, did he begin to achieve his vast potential. That season he had seven 200-plus-yard passing days and set club records for most passes attempted (369), most yards (2,489), and most completions (187) for 50.7 percent.

"Bart matured greatly that season," says his coach, Leeman Bennett. "He has learned that a quarterback can decide a game quicker than any other player on the field, and he is making the big play without making the big mistake. That comes only with experience, and now Bart has some."

O. J. SIMPSON

It isn't difficult to pick out O. J. Simpson's greatest day in football.

The day he surpassed Larry Brown in the last game of the 1972 season to win the National Football League rushing title?

No.

The day he set an NFL record with 250 yards in the opener of 1973?

Uh, uh.

The day he became the first player in pro football history to reach the 2,000-yard mark in a season?

Absolutely not.

All of the aforementioned would be pretty big days in anybody else's record book—but none are O. J.'s greatest.

His greatest day, he says, happened when he helped Southern Cal beat UCLA 21–20 in 1967, thereby claiming a Rose Bowl berth and no. 1 national ranking all in one glorious afternoon.

"For a single game, period, nothing could top that," Simpson says, "unless I have a great day in the Super Bowl."

Actually, that game *was* a college super bowl. It

matched the nation's no. 1 and no. 2 teams, bitter rivals from the same city, with the Rose Bowl and national championship at stake. As an added touch of glamor, both teams boasted the nation's leading Heisman Trophy candidates in Simpson and UCLA quarterback Gary Beban.

"You could not possibly have had a game that meant more to the people involved," says Simpson. "If both teams had lost nine of their previous games, that would still be the big game of the year. That game would have salvaged the season. But there we were, fighting not only for the championship of Los Angeles, but for no. 1 ranking in the nation as well."

Simpson scored two touchdowns that day, including one spectacular 64-yard run that provided the Trojans with their winning score in the last quarter. Ironically, Simpson was not in the mood to run at that particular moment because he was "too tired."

"I had just run the kickoff back and just carried the ball," recalls Simpson. "[Quarterback] Toby Page asked me if I could run again. I said, 'No.' I was breathing hard. So Page called a pass play.

"But the minute he got on the line, he changed it by audible and called my running play, the 23-Blast. And I figured, darn, what are you doing, Page? All I could do was react now. The ball was snapped, and I'm running the 23 and 64 yards later I'm in the end zone. And it turns out to be the biggest play of the year for us."

The game was clearly the highlight of Simpson's meteoric two-year career at Southern Cal.

Once an untamed youth in San Francisco's ghettoes, Simpson literally ran away from his past to become one of the nation's most honored football players. An exceptional two-year career at the City College of San Francisco, a junior college, established his credentials for Southern Cal. There he became coach John McKay's workhorse in 1967 and 1968, carrying the ball 674 times in that period for an average of 32 times a game. He established NCAA records for most yards rushing in a season (1,880 in 1968) and most gained in a career (3,540 in just two years). He also scored 36 touchdowns in that short period, winning the Heisman Trophy as the nation's best collegiate football player in 1968.

Simpson's qualities of speed and power made him an ideal combination of two backs. He could run outside like a halfback or inside like a fullback, and McKay rarely hesitated to use him in either capacity. "If you don't have O. J. carrying 35 to 40 times a game," pointed out the quick-witted McKay, "it would be like having Joe DiMaggio on your team and only letting him bat once a game."

A big day against Texas in the second game of the 1967 season, during which Simpson rushed for 164 yards, established a high profile for him on the national scene. Then he amassed 190 yards against Michigan State, 163 against Stanford, and 169 against Notre Dame. Simpson was injured late in the season but recuperated in time to play in the crucial UCLA game.

And what a game it was.

Beban showed why he was the class quarterback in the country, directing three UCLA touchdown drives. Simpson showed why he was the class tailback, flowing through UCLA defenders time and again for chunks of important yardage, despite playing on a throbbing, injured right foot that required a special sponge cover. It was Simpson's 13-yard touchdown run that provided the Trojans with a 14–7 lead at the half.

Later came what he considers the biggest play of his football career. With Southern Cal losing 20–14 as the result of Beban's second touchdown pass of the day, Simpson returned the kickoff and then ran two straight short-yardage plays.

"I was really kind of dragging," he says. "It wasn't that I didn't want the ball. [But] I had already carried some 30-odd times, and I just needed one play to get my wind. It happens a lot in pro and college ball. You know, give me one play to rest."

Page originally was not going to use Simpson for the play from the Southern Cal 36-yard line, but when the teams lined up, the quarterback noticed that UCLA defenders were anticipating his pass play. At this point he switched signals to the "23-Blast," a play whereby Simpson lined up deep and went through the left side of the line between guard and tackle. Simpson had heard it called many times during the 1967 season, and when it worked he could expect to get anywhere from 5 to 15 yards out of it.

But nobody expected what happened next.

Guard Steve Lehmer and tackle Mike Taylor cleared Simpson through a huge hole. One writer commented, "As it unfolded, it looked like maybe a five-yard gain." But then Simpson veered toward the left sideline, and the writer reappraised the situation: "Oh, well, a 15-yard gain and first down."

Suddenly, though, Trojan end Ron Drake was blocking out UCLA's defensive halfback, and the Bruin safety was cut out of the picture, too. And there was Simpson, turning toward the middle of the field, floating to his right, and nothing but open land appeared before him. Soon he was exerting his great speed, and the 90,000-plus fans in the Los Angeles Coliseum and millions more on national television knew he would not be brought down.

"Every time I think of that run," says Simpson, "I think about Muhammad Ali's fight [in 1964] with Sonny Liston. I could identify with Ali because he had reached a point in the fifth or sixth round where they had to push him out of the corner. Something was in his eyes and he didn't want to go out, and his handlers literally had to push him out. Two rounds later, he was champion of the world. Well, in that UCLA game, it was almost like they pushed me out of my corner. I was really straining. I was so tired after that run, all I could think of was: kick the extra point. The score was tied 20–20 at that point and we had to win the game to get to the Rose Bowl; we couldn't tie."

Rikki Aldridge (who will not be remembered as much as Simpson) then kicked the crucial tie-breaking extra point for the Trojans.

"It's funny," says Simpson. "There were still about seven minutes to go in the game, but it was about the fastest seven minutes I can ever remember. I think we went back on the field for one more series and the game was over. Even when the game was over, it was like I was waiting for Gary Beban to throw one of those miracle bombs he was famous for . . . especially against USC, which he had done on a few occasions."

There would be other elated moments for Simpson after he joined the pros.

"The last day of the 1972 NFL season, I gained 100 yards—you know, I've had better days—but I ended up leading the league in rushing," Simpson recalls. "I was second behind Larry Brown going into the game, and Larry got hurt. I can recall that being a big day."

Nor would Simpson forget the opener of 1973, when his Buffalo Bills played the New England Patriots and he broke the NFL record for rushing yardage in a game.

"We had lost six preseason games up to that time," Simpson says. "The Bills, in my professional career, had never won over four games in a season until that year. In that game against New England in Foxboro, I gained 250 yards, we won the opener, and it started what turned out to be my most successful season . . . and the Bills' first winning season since I was there. I think that game turned my pro career around, even though the year before I led the league in rushing and I was voted Most Valuable Player in the All-Star game . . . all of a sudden, you feel you've arrived. It was that day that I got my first NFL record, the Bills won the opening game, and it just sort of started what turned out to be two or three very satisfying years."

In the last game of the 1973 season, against the New York Jets in snow-covered Shea Stadium, Simpson broke Jimmy Brown's single-season rushing record of 1,863 yards. Simpson needed only 61 yards to break the record and wound up with a surplus. In fact, he not only smashed Brown's long-standing mark, he also broke ground previously untraveled by NFL runners in passing the 2,000-yard level. By the end of that 34–14 victory over the Jets, Simpson had totaled an incredible 2,003 yards for the season!

"When we came out on that field, there was no way I wasn't going to get the record," says Simpson. "I only needed 61 yards, and you know, I would have gotten it if I had had to carry the ball 67 times."

Simpson, of course, didn't need nearly that many carries to eclipse Brown's mark—and it was his thirty-fourth of the day, a seven-yard run, that brought him over the sacred 2,000-yard level.

"The guys carried me off into the locker room after I did it," recalls Simpson. "Then they left to go back to the game. There were still four minutes left . . . the longest four minutes I can recall in a game. I was in the locker room all by myself and I was just thinking, 'Two thousand yards! Wow. I gained 2,000 yards . . . I broke the record!' And everything went through my mind at that time . . . high school, Southern Cal, and of course I had had some rough years my first four years in Buffalo.

"And I thought about all the coaching changes we went through at that time and a public relations director we had in Buffalo, Jack Horrigan, who was dying of leukemia. When I was going through those tough times, getting to the point where I thought I couldn't stay in Buffalo anymore, he would say: 'You think you've got problems.' Of course I was aware of his situation and all. . . . He'd just say, 'Hey, you just stick it out and it will work out for you.' All these things went through my mind and made me feel glad that I was a football player and a Buffalo Bill.

"It was a feeling I don't think I could have gotten if I was drafted by the [Dallas] Cowboys or the [Los Angeles] Rams and accomplished the same thing. It dawned on me it meant that much more to me that it happened in Buffalo."

Simpson, of course, had not been particularly happy when he was drafted by the Bills. An NFL fan all his life (San Francisco and Los Angeles being classic NFL towns), he bridled a bit at the thought of going to an American Football League town.

"I had never really followed the AFL," he says. "Of course I knew nothing and nobody on the Buffalo Bills. There was never one person on that team that I had met even casually. On the other hand, I had many friends on NFL teams. It was also a part of the country that I knew nothing about.

"But, you know, I never complained that I was drafted by the Bills. The problem was I thought they weren't offering me a fair contract. I know I could have gotten more in Los Angeles or San Francisco. I guess morally it was hard for me to accept the fact that I was worth more to these teams, and I could get more from these teams, so why should I accept less from a team that I didn't particularly want to go to? Now if I could have gone there without the penalty of less money, I don't think you would have seen any hesitation."

It would take some time before Simpson got adjusted to the new surroundings. But this warm-blooded, Southern California product finally began to flower in Buffalo's icy environs by 1972. And by 1973 he was bursting out all over, thanks to a gallant offensive line.

"Some of these guys had been maligned," said Simpson, "but they worked hard and did the job. I mean, they really did the job. We were running the ball at teams who knew we were running. We were only throwing three, four passes a game. And these guys still came through. I've never in my football career seen, let alone been a part of, such closeness and camaraderie between a group of guys. I'm sure in 1983 we'll have a ten-year reunion somewhere. If things are going well with me, I'll see to it."

In a typical gesture befitting his noble character, Simpson insisted that the players on the Bills' superb offensive line stand up and be counted with him at a press conference on the day after he reached the 2,000-yard mark. Then, on television he introduced each player by name.

Simpson puts that day right up there with the best of them. But great as it was, it falls yards short of one golden afternoon in the California sunshine.

"I know somebody's going to come along and break the 2,000-yard record," says Simpson. "It's going to happen soon, especially with the new 16-game season. Sooner or later, pro records fall. But what happened in the Southern Cal-UCLA game in 1967, well, I know that's something they'll still be talking about at USC 20 or 30 years from now."

LENNY MOORE

The "greatest" football game in Baltimore Colts history was played in 1958. No, it wasn't the one you think. It happened several weeks earlier, according to Lenny Moore.

"Everybody talks about the 1958 championship game with the New York Giants as being a great game," says Moore, "but the game with San Francisco earlier in the season was a better game team-wise. We should have blown the Giants out in that world championship game. We had them well under control . . . it wasn't as close as the final score indicated."

If it hadn't been for Baltimore's Western Division-clinching victory over San Francisco that season, there might never have been that so-called "greatest game ever played" in which the Colts beat the Giants 23–17 in overtime for the National Football League championship.

In order to beat San Francisco, the Colts had to come back from a 20-point deficit at the half—something they had never accomplished in their history!

The day was November 30, 1958.

"We were losing 27–7 at the half to the 49ers," Moore remembers. "We were favored to win, but we just couldn't get things rolling at the start. Y. A. Tittle was hot—he was killing us.

"Strange, though. We weren't down mentally when we went into the locker room at halftime. There wasn't any kind of frustration that you would normally have being down by that much. No, we just calmly sat there and said, 'We're going to stick with our game plan. We just have to execute a little better.' There was calmness there. We just said, 'Hey, come on, let's put it together. We can get these guys.'"

And they did.

Point by point, the Colts caught up with the 49ers, and Moore had the personal satisfaction of finally putting his team ahead, at 28–27, with a 73-yard touchdown run.

Final score: Baltimore 35, San Francisco 27.

Everything was stacked in San Francisco's favor in the first half: 27–7 in points and 231–92 in the yardage statistics. The second half was different, though, with Baltimore scoring 28 points to none for San Francisco and holding a 313–87 advantage in yardage.

You couldn't have blamed any of the chilled 57,557 fans in Baltimore's Memorial Stadium, though, if they had quit at the half. It certainly looked as if their beloved Colts had done just that. Tittle had split the Colt defense wide open, twice directing 80-yard touchdown drives and capping both with rollouts. The 49ers also scored on Hugh McElhenny's one-yard plunge and Matt Hazletine's 13-yard interception return of a deflected Johnny Unitas pass. The only Baltimore score of the first half had been on a 65-yard drive capped by a Unitas sprintout.

In the Baltimore locker room during halftime, coach Weeb Ewbank stalked to the blackboard and scrawled in large letters: "WE NEED FOUR TOUCHDOWNS." Then, in more precise terms, he told his team how to get them: Be content to keep the pass patterns short, and just keep picking away.

The Colts followed his advice for the most part. Unitas first took them on a 62-yard, 13-play drive capped by Alan "The Horse" Ameche's one-yard plunge. At this moment, it was announced that the Pittsburgh Steelers had upset the Chicago Bears, leaving the Western Division title open for the Colts if they could grab it. It seemed like an inspirational message from above to Baltimore safety Ray Brown, who intercepted a pass intended for R. C. Owens in the end zone. This gave the Colts possession on their own 20.

Baltimore was on the move again, this time a 50-yard pass from Unitas to Jim Mutscheller highlighting a long scoring drive. Ameche once again scored from the one-yard line to cut the 49ers' lead to 27–21, and the Memorial Stadium crowd became a roaring madhouse.

Later Unitas pitched to Moore, and he went 73 yards for the go-ahead touchdown. Blocks by Art Spinney and Ameche set him loose, and Moore got escort help later on downfield from George Preas. Steve Myhra's extra-point kick gave the Colts the lead at 28–27.

"It was sort of a sweep play to the left," Moore recalls. "We kind of broke it inside the linebacker. It was Matt Hazletine who came across for them and we kicked him out, and I cut up in between and then toward the sidelines. And we had blockers downfield and I just kind of maneuvered in and around my downfield blockers."

This is the way Unitas described the key play in the *Baltimore Morning Sun:*

"I lined Moore up at halfback and called a sweep to the left. Nothing fancy, just a straight power sweep. Moore took the handoff. The left guard and tackle, Art Spinney and Jim Parker, collapsed the 49er line. Ameche threw a block and Moore turned the corner. [Raymond] Berry threw a block. Moore twisted away from the cornerback, cut back toward the middle of the field and followed Preas."

The Colts finished their miracle comeback when Unitas later threw a touchdown pass to Berry to cap an 11-play drive that was set up by Carl Taseff's interception. A story goes along with that last play, according to Bill Tanton of the *Baltimore Evening Sun*.

"During the decisive drive, the Colts had a third and long situation on their own 40," Tanton writes. "Johnny Unitas called time out and went to the sidelines to get a play from Ewbank.

" 'What have you got, Weeb?' asked Unitas.

" 'What have you got, John?' Ewbank asked back.

" 'What have I got?' snapped Unitas. 'You're the coach. I want you to help us with a play.'

"Ewbank turned away from Unitas and walked around in a little circle," Tanton said. "The people in the stands watched anxiously. Then they saw Weeb go to Unitas with the answer.

" 'Get a first down,' said Ewbank.

"Unitas went out on the field and called his own play, a pass, and it went for a touchdown and the Colts lived happily ever after," Tanton related. "Art Donovan [a Colts Hall of Famer] swears Weeb turned to acknowledge the cheers of the crowd, which thought Ewbank's genius had led to the TD."

As the game was drawing to a close, Baltimore fans began spilling out of the stands and were lining all four sides of the field when the final gun sounded. They flooded the playing field then and lifted several of the Baltimore players on their shoulders for a ride to the locker room.

It was the beginning of a wild ride for the Baltimore Colts, who at this point in history began raising their own profile and that of pro football in general. The Colts won consecutive world championships in 1958 and 1959 and had a personal hand in the so-called "golden age" of pro football. The championship game with the Giants in 1958, especially, might have done more public relations work for football than any other in history.

"I think pro football really came into prominence after that 1958 world championship game," says Moore. "It meant the real big introduction of television and the first sudden-death overtime game. From then on, financially and everything else, football became a success. The television contracts got bigger and bigger with that game. It all points back to that championship game, really, with that exposure. That's probably why they say that game turned professional football around."

The quality of those Baltimore Colts teams had something to do with pro football's sparkling new image, too.

"As I reflect back on it," Moore says, "we would probably go down as one of the greatest teams in football history. The thing is, offensively and defensively, we had so many outstanding guys. Someone was always coming up with a super play defensively, enough to stop a drive here or a pass there. Offensively, we hit from any point on the field. It wasn't a question of just plodding it down the field and banging our heads against the wall. Look around and Unitas would hit Raymond Berry with a pass and Raymond may go 30 or 40 yards. He may hit me and I may go 50. We'd have a draw play and I'd be able to run it through. Whatever . . . we could attack from any point on the field. And that's what kept the other defense loose, because they didn't know what to expect. Johnny, only the way he could, mixed his plays, and the way he mixed them kept the defense off balance."

Not surprisingly, all seven Baltimore players now in the Hall of Fame were part of those great late-'50s teams: Unitas, Moore, Berry, Donovan (a defensive tackle), Jim Parker (a guard and tackle), Gino Marchetti (a defensive end), and coach Ewbank. Few of them played a greater role than Moore in the success of those dynastic Baltimore teams.

A high-profile runner at Penn State in his college days, Moore was Baltimore's first-round draft choice in

1956 after the Colts discussed his potential with Joe Paterno, the Nittany Lions' assistant coach at the time. Paterno told them: "Go tell Weeb Ewbank not to miss this guy, because if he does, it will be the greatest mistake he could ever make."

Paterno's advice was right on the money. Moore, used as a combination flanker and running back, was the NFL's Rookie of the Year in 1956 and went on to pile up impressive statistics in a 12-year career as the Colts enjoyed some of their finest seasons. He retired in 1967 with 11,213 combined net yards, including 5,174 rushing and 363 pass receptions for 6,039 yards. In addition, he scored 678 points on 113 touchdowns, including stretches of 18 straight games where he scored at least one touchdown, and 11 straight where he had at least one TD rushing. Both of those marks are NFL records.

In 1964 Moore was given the dual honor of the NFL's Most Valuable Player and Comeback Player of the Year, a personal distinction he enjoyed above all his others.

"That was the most meaningful season for me because I overcame some adversity to do it," Moore says. "Some people were saying that I had slowed down and that I was through. I had something to prove to them and to myself. I kind of dedicated myself to that year; I said, 'I'll show 'em.' I put everything else aside and devoted myself to nothing else but that year. And that was the most satisfying of all my years in football."

Ironically, just before his greatest season the Colts had tried to trade off Moore. Due to a switch in the Colts' offensive style and a rash of injuries to the aging star, Moore became relatively ineffective in the early 1960s. An emergency appendectomy just prior to the 1963 season put him out of action for two games. Then he missed the last five with a head injury.

However, he reported to training camp the following season in top physical condition for the first time in several years. And not long thereafter, he was off and running. In the second game of the season, coach Don Shula inserted Moore into the lineup against Green Bay, and almost immediately he scored on a 58-yard pass play from Unitas. Later he took the ball over for the winning touchdown as the Colts defeated the Western Division favorites, 21–20. Moore once again was the game-breaker with two TDs as the Colts beat the Packers 24–21 later in the season and clinched a divisional crown.

Moore later retired from football grudgingly.

"I wasn't ready to quit in 1967," he told the *Baltimore Sun*. "I was only 33. The Colts had just added Timmy Brown to replace me at halfback but I went to Don Shula and said, 'Hey, I can still do it as a wide receiver.' But he wouldn't go for it. I didn't know it could all end so quickly. You're a hero one day, a forgotten man the next."

Some remembered, though. Moore was given a chance as a television sportscaster on CBS, and later he became promotions director for the Colts, his present job. Old halfbacks don't fade away, it seems—they just move into other positions.

ARCHIE MANNING

Because of the heat he was getting from all sides, figuratively and literally, Archie Manning will always remember his first game in the National Football League.

The year before, he was the glamor player of college football at Mississippi, and his acquisition by the New Orleans Saints triggered a new high in optimism there. Many thought this dandy young quarterback would be the Saints' savior.

"I had been their no. 1 draft choice," Manning recalls. "I was the second person taken in the draft. The Saints had traded off Billy Kilmer the year before, you know, to get me. So it was kind of like, well, we have this kid from Ole Miss here and he's going to save the franchise. I mean, everyone was saying, here's the guy who's going to do it for us. I think even my teammates must've thought I was some kind of superman."

But they found out that Manning was only human after all, as he ran into contract problems and then an injury that kept him out of most of the 1971 preseason games.

"I was late for signing," says Manning, "so I didn't play in the first preseason game. I played in half of the second one, started the third one against Kansas City, and got hurt. I didn't play again until the last preseason game against Houston."

The Houston game, as were the previous exhibition contests, turned out to be a losing effort. So the Saints went into the 1971 season with an 0–6 record in preseason play and the definite role of the underdog.

The prospects for the season were scary, Manning remembers, especially since the Saints had to open against the powerful Los Angeles Rams.

"At that time," Manning says, "the Rams were right up there with the San Francisco 49ers in the Western Division [of the National Conference] and Roman Gabriel was still the quarterback. They still had a great defense with people like Coy Bacon, Merlin Olson, Deacon Jones. Marlin McKeever was still one of the league's top linebackers. Kermit Alexander was still playing . . . so they had a really good ballclub.

"We had about 14 rookies on our squad, and I guess probably the only player that anyone ever heard of on our team at that time was [receiver] Danny Abramowicz."

A near-capacity crowd of 70,915 was on hand in Tulane Stadium to watch the Saints' new wonder boy. Little did they know, though, that he almost didn't start the game because of a combination of circumstances.

"I had been kind of a running quarterback in college," says Manning, "so I went out before the game to do some running. I was all pumped up. My adrenalin was flowing, and I did a lot of running before the game. I did a couple of two, three, four-hundred yard runs and then a couple of forties. You know, I figured I would have to do some running that day with that front four that Los Angeles had, and I really wanted to get my legs good and loose. And I also threw a lot of passes in practice.

"Well, by the time I went into the locker room right before the game, I was just totally exhausted. As we were coming out onto the field, I felt I was going to have to tell the trainer I couldn't go. I had some cramps in my stomach, too, I guess from nervousness, but I didn't say anything to the trainer because of embarrassment. The biggest fear of my life was having to tell the coach, or the trainer, that I didn't think I could play."

The weather conditions that day didn't help any, either.

"It was just unbelievably hot," Manning recalls. "The humidity in New Orleans can be just incredible. It was the hottest ballgame I've ever played in. They had just installed artificial turf in Tulane Stadium, and the sun bouncing off it must have made the field about 127 degrees. The sun magnifies tremendously on a surface like that. It rained at halftime and then it rained again in the second half, but the sun came out again and it was as hot as ever. I know the Los Angeles Rams were just drained from the heat. Merlin Olson and Deacon Jones were having spells and had to be sent in and out of the game at various intervals. And I remember they had a linebacker, Jim Purnell, he almost died after the game. They had to bring him into our dressing room and plug him into an oxygen machine. He was just white as a sheet. It was really dangerous."

Not helping matters any for Manning was the ferocious Los Angeles defensive line, which sacked the brand-new Saints quarterback six times in the first half. But Manning made up for it with a great second half. He wound up the game completing 16 of 29 passes for 218 yards and one touchdown, to Dave Parks. Abramowicz, who had not done much preseason business, caught five of Manning's passes this day for 73 yards.

It was a tight, but sane, first half with each team having only a field goal to show for its sweat. Skip Butler kicked a 32-yarder for New Orleans, and David Ray hit one 31 yards for Los Angeles, both in the second period.

Manning, whose passing in the first half had resulted

in minus yardage (a first for the franchise), was a different quarterback in the second. On the Saints' first possession of the third quarter, Manning moved them downfield in a hurry, passing 12 yards to Bob Newland, 21 to Parks, and then 22 to Abramowicz for a first down at the Los Angeles 18. Five plays later, with the help of a great catch by Bob Gresham, Manning had the Saints in the end zone with a six-yard rollout pass to Parks.

With the help of a fumble by Gabriel at the Los Angeles six-yard line, the Saints had another touchdown less than three minutes later. Rich Neal recovered for New Orleans, and three plays later Gresham dashed two yards into the end zone for a 17–3 Saints lead. The frantic third period finished shortly after Ray's 27-yard field goal for Los Angeles had cut New Orleans' lead to 17–6.

At this point the Rams were exhausted from the heat, but not dead. They quickly took advantage of an intercepted Manning pass to score a touchdown early in the fourth period. Gabriel, perking up after a flat three quarters, completed a 29-yard touchdown pass play to Les Josephson to trim the Saints' lead to 17–13. And the next time the Rams got the ball, they drove 63 yards in 11 plays, the last one a one-yard touchdown plunge by Josephson. Ray's extra point gave the Rams a 20–17 lead with less than five minutes remaining in the game.

The score was still the same with 1:24 to go, with the ball in the Saints' possession resting on their own 30-yard line. Manning didn't have much time for a miracle.

"We called a sprintout play," Manning remembers, "and I hit Gresham for a good chunk of yardage."

The pass play went for 37 yards up the middle to the Los Angeles 33. Now there was 1:10 left.

"Then I hit Abramowicz with a sideline pass, and I hit Abramowicz later again and got an interference call."

Manning's pass for Abramowicz at the right corner of the end zone had been overthrown, but Jim Nettles was called for defensive interference. That put the ball on the Los Angeles one with 23 seconds remaining.

"We tried a running play and didn't get much," says Manning. "Time was running out and I used my last timeout with three seconds to go. I went over to the sideline to talk it over [with coach J. D. Roberts]. Of course the decision was whether to take a field goal and take a tie, or go for it from the one."

As it turned out, Manning never got a decisive answer from Roberts.

"It's ironic," Manning says, now chuckling. "I had gone over to the sidelines, and we were talking about two or three different plays we might run. But before we could make a decision, they came and got me back on the field, and the coaches never did tell me which play to run. So when I went back in, I reverted back to my college days and ran a sprintout . . . you know, a run-pass option. Actually, I don't think I ever thought about passing it. I turned it up and cut across the goal and as soon as I hit the goal, I fumbled. It was a little scary at first. I didn't know whether I had actually scored or not. I just lay on the ground and waited for the reaction of the crowd. Fortunately, it was loud and we had beaten them."

Manning remembers that the Rams "protested strongly" about the suspect touchdown play, but to no avail. The final gun went off, with the Saints winning 24 –20.

"It was just an unbelievable first game for me," Manning says. "My statistics were fairly good, and on top of that, we had beaten a great team in Los Angeles."

For a rookie in his first NFL game, Manning also had held his mistakes to a minimum—even if his coach did not think so. Remembers the quarterback:

"My offensive coordinator was a guy named Ken Shipp, an old, slow-talking southern guy who smoked a pipe. I remember on Monday, the day after the game, he told me: 'Damn, son, we had 69 plays and you made four mistakes.' They were quarterback mistakes, not necessarily interceptions, but four things where I perhaps should have checked off, didn't do this or that. I was calling my own plays. The ironic thing about it was that I probably played about seven more years before I had another game where I made that few mistakes. But I set some sort of precedent for myself that I wasn't able to repeat. Game after game, it got a lot tougher after that. I really mean it."

Playing under what he calls "an awful lot of pressure" because of his position as the team's no. 1 draft choice, Manning took some time before blossoming into an NFL star. He did have one solid year in his second season, 1972, when he completed 51.3 percent of his passes for 2,781 yards and ran for 351 more. But it wasn't until 1978 that he realized his potential. That year he completed 291 of 471 passes, an excellent 61.8 percent, for 3,416 yards and 17 TDs. In addition, he ran for 202 yards more. He capped the season with numerous awards, including Player of the Year in the National Conference, and in the Pro Bowl he was instrumental in a 13–7 victory for the NFC.

If anyone has come a long way, it's Manning, often referred to as a "Huck Finn in shoulder pads" because of his freckled, All-American-boy look.

"I kind of magnified the pressure on me at the start," he says. "I had contract trouble and couldn't get together with the team. I didn't even go to the college All-Star game because I hadn't signed. Coach Roberts was going to play me, there wasn't any doubt about it. But I had not played in any kind of pro system in college; it was all new to me, as far as reading the defenses and reading zone coverages and man-to-man, and checking off. It was really different than the college system I had known, so it was a lot of pressure."

So there was Archie Manning, college whiz at Ole

Miss, quarterback of the quarter century (1950–75) in the Southeastern Conference, thrown right into the professional fires in 1971 against the mighty Los Angeles Rams.

Luckily for him, things fell into place, including his passes.

"Our defense was playing well that day," Manning recalls of his first game, "and the Rams were kind of struggling. Gabriel, I remember, didn't have a good day for them. They were much superior to us in talent, really. But things happened for us; like, we were down on the ten-yard line and I threw a pass up the middle and it got tipped in the air, just a sure interception ball. One of my players [Gresham] and one of their players [Marlin McKeever] both went up for it. You know, it was really tipped high. It was like a jump ball in basketball and they both came down with it. It was a wrestling match, and we got the ball and went on in and scored. That's the kind of luck we needed for a game like that."

BILL BERGEY

For more than a decade, Jim Otto had been making an impact on the National Football League. This specific day, Bill Bergey wanted to make an impact on Jim Otto.

"I had seen a lot of film on the Oakland Raiders and I had watched Otto," says Bergey. "I was completely awed by the man because he simply never made a mistake. So I went into the ballgame just saying if I could do anything at all against him, I should feel very, very lucky. . . ."

The year was 1969 and Bergey was just a rookie linebacker for the Cincinnati Bengals. Otto, of course, was an established star at the time for the Oakland Raiders, having been an All-Pro center in the NFL for as long as Bergey could remember.

The two met officially for the first time at Nippert Stadium on the campus of the University of Cincinnati. "It was a rainy, nasty, miserable day," Bergey recalls, "and we were playing the 4–3 defense where I was the middle linebacker right across from Otto. I was so fired up, so hyper, and so excited that I just kept saying, try to make anything happen against Otto, anything at all."

Bergey surpassed his wildest dreams this day.

"I got to the point where I was making a lot of plays, and I was making a lot of tackles and I couldn't believe what was happening. The score at the half was 24–0 in our favor and I had come up with some big plays and caused a lot of turnovers."

Even more surprising was a 31–17 victory for the Bengals, an upstart expansion team. It was the only loss that year for the powerful Raiders, the evergreens of the American Conference.

"That was the year they went 12–1–1 and we were the only team to beat them," underscores Bergey. "I mean, we really whipped them bad."

But the game also is memorable to Bergey for one other reason: an incident with Otto.

"I guess it was about halfway through the fourth period and John Madden [the Oakland coach] knew that I was getting the best of Otto," says Bergey. "One time he had chased me all the way to the sidelines and I had tackled a guy for a one-yard loss, and Madden said, 'Come on, Otto, get to him.' And I looked up at Madden and said, 'He's not fast enough.' Well, you don't say something like that about a guy who's made All-Pro 12 years in a row.

"So with about two minutes left in the ballgame, they had thrown a screen pass. They got the ball about 30 yards down the field, and a receiver had fumbled the ball, and one of our players, Fletcher Smith, a defensive back, recovered it. I slid in over Fletcher, just kind of hovered over him to make sure that he had the ball. Well, by that time, Jim Otto had started a 30-yard sprint for my jaw and hit me really hard. Watching the films, it looked like my head left my shoulders. It was an illegal shot, of course, a 15-yard penalty, all because of what I had said before about him not being fast enough. You know, I was just a little, spunky rookie and rookies aren't very highly thought of by the veterans, especially a guy who's made All-Pro so many years."

Bergey, feeling sick, wandered over to the sidelines with a little help from his friends.

"The doctor was moving his finger from one side to the other in front of my face," Bergey remembers, "and I saw about five fingers."

That night, Bergey went back to his apartment with his roommate, Guy Dennis, and went to sleep. "But about two or three in the morning, I woke up with the worst headache anyone could imagine," says Bergey. "We didn't have any aspirin in the house, so we had to drive to the other side of town to wake up some friends for medication. Well, I got four Bufferin tablets from my friends and went back to sleep. I woke up the next morning about seven-thirty or eight o'clock and I felt like a million dollars, and I had to smile to myself about that game, even though Otto had taken that cheap shot at me."

Otto later apologized to Bergey for the blow, but that wasn't the entire finish of the incident.

"It was such a cheap shot," says Bergey, "that my linebacker coach, Vince Costello, said to me: 'The next time you get a crack at him, you take it.' So I did take my shot at him a year later, but you just kind of forget about it after that."

Even after a decade of retrospect, Bergey is still incredulous over his performance that day.

"I look back and I think about that game, and there's no question in my mind it was my best day in the NFL," says Bergey, an All-Pro linebacker himself with the Philadelphia Eagles now. "I know I didn't score a touchdown with an interception or anything like that, but I must have had close to 20 tackles that day. I had an absolute field day against Jim Otto, probably the greatest center I've ever played against. Knowing how good that man was, it was an unbelievable thing for a rookie to do."

Bergey recalls that it was "probably the hardest-hitting game I've ever been in. At the beginning of the second half, we scored another touchdown, so it was 31–0, and here we were an expansion club just kicking the hell out of this powerhouse Oakland Raider team. And we were all fired up. It was really a dandy."

Bergey was officially credited with ten unassisted tackles this day, not to mention many others that he was in on.

"When I went into this game, I was so shook and scared," he says. "But it's funny, when I was down there in my stance I just felt like I was going to make every tackle."

Born and raised in South Dayton, N. Y., Bergey was a Little All-American at Arkansas State and regarded as the best football player in the school's history. A second-round draft choice of the Bengals in 1969, Bergey really came into his own after he was traded to the Eagles for three draft choices in 1974. In Philadelphia he became a perennial Pro Bowl player and All-Pro, ranking with Hall of Famer Chuck Bednarik as one of the greatest linebackers in Eagles history.

Until a knee injury early in the 1979 season knocked him out of action for the year, Bergey was a virtual "Six Million Dollar Man" for the Eagles, starting in all 75 games since coming to Philadelphia. That made 141 starts out of a possible 142 in 11 years for him.

When Bergey was finally put on his back, the Eagles were incredulous. Said quarterback Ron Jaworski: "I couldn't believe Bill was hurt. I had never seen him in the trainer's room. His ability to avoid clean licks was amazing. There were people going at his legs all the time and he'd never get hurt."

Bergey had been injured before, but never enough to keep him out of a game. One time he suffered a compound dislocation of his thumb during a contest, but he yanked it back in place himself, had a cast placed on it, and continued playing.

Explaining his ability to stay on his feet for a decade in the NFL, Bergey once said: "I feel like I've got a knack to roll with a play. I can almost act like a drunk and go limp. Instead of fighting a hit, I roll with it."

Ironically, it was this inability to "roll with it" against the New Orleans Saints that resulted in his disabling injury.

"This time," explains Bergey, "I had my feet planted in the Astroturf. Conrad Dobler hit me up high, a clean shot, but I couldn't pick my foot up off the turf. It was locked. Astroturf is a filthy, terrible thing to play on."

That savage blow put Bergey down, but not out.

"I'm not going to use this injury as an excuse to retire," he says, "because I'm going to come back and play three or four more years."

No game in Philadelphia was perhaps more reflective of Bergey's talents than one against San Francisco in 1974, when he had two interceptions and two fumble recoveries. In fact, that probably ranks as his "second greatest game," and for more than one reason.

"The oddity about it," says Bergey, "is that as I was leaving home for the game, I told my wife, Micky, that I felt I was going to have a really big one this particular weekend. And I gave her a kiss and told her I was going to get an interception for her. I gave my oldest boy, Jason, a kiss, too, and said I was going to get him an interception. And I kissed the younger boy, Jake, my baby, and said I was going to get him a fumble recovery, and get one for me, too. [At the time, Bergey had two children. Now he has three, with the addition of Joshua.]

"Well, that's exactly what happened. It was the only time in my career that I had ever said anything like that before a game, you know, called the shots and had them all come true. I had told my neighbor what I had done before I left for the ballpark, and after the game he gave me four mugs, one for each of my family, with a perso-

nalized inscription on them saying, 'The interception for
you, Micky,' the date, the score of the game, and so
forth.

"I still have them up in the kitchen on the shelf, and
I look at them every day I come into the house."

REGGIE McKENZIE

Anonymity usually being a condition of National Football League linemen, Reggie McKenzie gets his kicks when he can.

"You just have to get a lot of personal satisfaction out of getting the job done," says the Buffalo Bills' All-Pro guard. "People in the game might appreciate good quality offensive linemen, but few others know their names."

Perhaps McKenzie's high-profile days aren't universally recognized, but he knows when he turns in a Hall of Fame game—like the time he helped O. J. Simpson reach the 2,000-yard rushing plateau in the last contest of the 1973 season.

"It will always stand out in my mind as being the biggest game I ever played in," says McKenzie. "From every aspect: emotionally, I was very happy about the moment, happy for O. J.; spiritually, I was happy about the team coming together."

McKenzie, a 6′4″, 240-pounder out of Michigan, was part of a proud unit called "The Electric Company"—the Bills' offensive line so named because it "turned on the Juice." The "Juice," of course, was Simpson.

The Bills' offensive line lived up to its flashy nickname (coined by public relations director J. Budd Thalman) throughout the 1973 season, leading the ubiquitous Simpson on his record-breaking trail. The group was a combination of bits and pieces put together by an astute front office. McKenzie, for one, was drafted out of Michigan on the second round in 1972.

"Guys at Michigan told me I was going to Buffalo and I didn't believe it, because I thought I would go in the first round to some other team," remembers McKenzie. "The Bills had already made their first-round pick." As it was, McKenzie was later picked by the Bills, the twenty-eighth player selected in the draft.

The next year the Bills picked up Mike Montler in a trade with New England and converted the guard-tackle to a center. Then they got guard Joe DeLamielleure and tackle Paul Seymour in the draft and obtained tackle Dave Foley on injured waivers from the New York Jets. The Bills already had another capable tackle on the team in Donnie Green, so Seymour was made a tight end. Thus, "The Electric Company" was formed, and for sheer electricity, no NFL lines could equal it. Says McKenzie: "We went strong side, right off tackle, you know, 'Here we come!' "

With a fine offensive line like that, not only did Simpson become the first player in NFL history to reach 2,000 rushing yards in a season, but the team became the first one to hit the 3,000-yard mark. McKenzie credits offensive coach Jim Ringo for most of that success.

"Ringo provided us with an ideal running attack," says McKenzie. "He brought O. J. out of the I formation and just had him picking his hole, and he had some fantastic plays. That was Ringo's style, that Green Bay Packer-type attack, and it really blended in well." (Ringo had played for the championship Packer teams of the late 1960s that had featured the famed power sweep led by Jerry Kramer, among others.)

As for McKenzie's most personally satisfying day, the story must go back to 1972, when he first got acquainted with Simpson in his rookie year.

"I tell you when I first came to Buffalo, I just couldn't believe the talent Simpson had as a running back," McKenzie says. "I came from Michigan, and with Bo Schembechler, we used to run the ball all the time. And I had never seen talent like O. J.'s before. In my first year, he got his first 1,000 yards [in one season] as a pro, and I couldn't believe it. I thought surely he must have done it before. It was in Cleveland, it was in the mud . . . I'll never forget . . . because we didn't win but four games that year, and he came in, we lost the game, but he was kind of feeling good. 'Yeah, I got a 1,000 yards,'' Simpson said. And I said, 'Man, is that the first time you got 1,000 yards?' He told me, 'First time.' I said, 'I can't believe it.' I said, 'You can do better than that . . . We'll do better than that next year.' "

During the off-season McKenzie and Simpson intensified their relationship.

"I went out and spent a little time at his place in California," says McKenzie, "and we just firmed up a real good friendship. During the course of the off-season, we would call each other. I was living in Michigan at the time. We would call back and forth to each other and see how each other was doing in terms of working out. And I was dreaming about the season coming up; I was working out and I was really excited, saving my energy for the new season. And I told O. J., 'You can get 2,000 yards.' And he kind of paused. He didn't believe it. And I said again, 'You can do 2,000.' And he said, 'Well, maybe 1,500.' And I said, 'No, you can do 2,000.'

"And as the season started, we were playing New England and he rushed for 250 yards. He was just elated. The next week we played the San Diego Chargers and he got 103 yards. And then we opened our own stadium with the New York Jets and he went for 123 yards. I'll never forget, I was sitting in a car with O. J. and his wife after the game and I said, 'Two thousand,' you know, to

remind him. And he kind of looked at me with a
sheepish grin and said, 'Well, maybe 1,600.' "

Perhaps Simpson was saying '1,600,' but he was no
doubt thinking '2,000' midway through the season as he
continued to pile up yardage. Simpson gained 171 yards
against the Philadelphia Eagles and 166 against the Baltimore Colts, and McKenzie remembers that O. J. told
him: "I'm going to have a treat for Howard Cosell on
the Monday night football game—1,000 yards in seven
games."

"And that's exactly what he did," says McKenzie,
"but like I said, the whole season was phenomenal."

After a 157-yard performance against the Kansas City
Chiefs in the seventh game of the season—exactly the
halfway point—Buffalo's talented back was up to 1,025
yards. And Buffalo's talented line was starting to get the
recognition it deserved, especially from Simpson who,
full of praises, continued to publicly pat his teammates
on their strong backs.

The marvelous oxen on Buffalo's offensive line, led by
the inspired McKenzie, continued to pull for Simpson.
The yardage continued to pile up, and after a 219-yard
day against New England in the thirteenth game of the
year, Simpson had amassed 1,803 yards. He needed just
61 yards in the last game, against the New York Jets, to
surpass Jimmy Brown's single-season rushing record,
and 197 to reach the coveted 2,000-yard level.

Simpson knew it was in sight now. More importantly,
so did McKenzie and his broad-shouldered teammates
on the Buffalo line.

"The dramatics for that day began building during
the week," says McKenzie. "The media was of course
building up the 61 yards needed for Jimmy Brown's
record and then the quest of 2,000 yards. To me, that
was the ultimate. We had an offensive day on Wednes-
day, a defensive day on Thursday, and Friday we pretty
much didn't do anything at all. Because we had become

very close, the offensive line as a group used to sit and just have meetings with the running backs. And after practice—I'll never forget because it was cold and everyone was tired and really wanted to get the season over with—the offensive line went down as a group to look at game films.

"There was myself, Mike Montler, Joe De-Lamielleure, Donnie Green, Dave Foley, and Paul Seymour. We watched an extra can of film on the Jets. We sat in there and just kind of talked about the plays, and how we were going to block them, and what to anticipate so we would have communication among ourselves. Everyone else on the team was leaving, but the offensive line stayed late that day. We were determined."

That Sunday, their determination was evident.

"Everybody put their heads in there and just kind of looked at each other," McKenzie says. "And we said to ourselves, we're not to be denied. From that point on, it was in us. We were going out to get the record for O. J. and of course win the football game. And the way we were rolling, nobody was going to stop us.

"The first play of the game, we ran a "26," which is a play that O. J. never thought would work. Jim Ringo put it in for O. J. I remember in 1972 Ringo told him: 'I've got a play for you and it can go all the way.' We practiced it, but O. J. thought it would never go. In the play, O. J. would be going strong side. The tight end would be on the right side and what we called the 'on guard' would pull out of the line and kick out the linebacker, and O. J. would read the guard's block. If he kicked him out, O. J. took it up in the hole; if he pinned him, he came outside.

"Well, we were playing Pittsburgh in War Memorial Stadium when we called the '26.' We went around right end . . . O. J. went 94 yards for the score, in the mud, yet. And when he came off the field, he hugged Jim

Ringo, and ever since then he's been a big fan of that play."

Simpson didn't get 94 yards against the Jets with the "26," but he did do plenty of damage, McKenzie recalls.

"I think he got 44 yards on it. But O. J. could have gone all the way on that first play and broken Jimmy Brown's record right then and there, except he fell down in the snow. It was kind of wet at Shea Stadium. After that he went on and got the 61 yards. He was happy about that. But I think his determination really came out when he went after the 2,000-yard record, because then he knew it was in sight. He knew he would have to have a terrific day to make it . . . and that's what he had."

Simpson made it on his thirty-fourth carry of the day, a play that is forever branded in McKenzie's memory.

"It was a similar play to the '26,' " he remembers. "It was called a '27.' I was the 'on guard' on this play. It was strong left. I pulled out, pinned the linebacker, and Joe DeLamielleure took it outside, and O. J. scooted up in between, and that was the 2,000 yards."

The officials stopped the game at this point and handed Simpson the ball. Then his teammates carried Simpson off the field into the locker room, where he remained alone for the last four minutes of the game to savor his impossible dream season.

"After O. J. got the 2,000 yards," says McKenzie, "I remember it was kind of still for a moment. Then someone said, 'Carry that man off the field.' And the fellows on the sidelines went out and picked him up . . . it was touching . . . it was touching . . . I've got a copy of that highlight film. The way the announcer did it, it really got to you."

Simpson later showed yards of class when he had his offensive line stand up and take a bow before reporters and television cameras. McKenzie remembers this as a touching moment, too:

"O. J. was just showing his appreciation for what a good offensive line can do for a running back. Here he was, coming out of Southern Cal as the back of the decade, yet it took him six years to get a 1,000-yard season. He had always had confidence in himself that he could do it, but he just never had the supporting cast. And when he got the group, the 'Company,' he wanted to share it with us, and he wanted to let the other backs in the NFL know that you've got to have people up front."

Now that they were "television personalities," the faces on "The Electric Company" became clearer in the public's view. Points out McKenzie:

"Nobody expected us to do much of anything, but that day—and that year—was just a takeoff for everybody's career on that offensive line. It finally happened for O. J., and it finally happened for us, too."

"The Electric Company" has just about gone out of business since then, though. Green and Montler were traded in 1977. In 1978 Dave Foley retired. Simpson's last year with the Bills came after the 1977 season, when he was traded to San Francisco.

" 'The Electric Company' was still respected after that great year," McKenzie notes, "because O. J. got 1,000 yards in 1976. But the intensity we had as a team was lost, because of moves that management had made. O. J. became disgruntled, and you could say he was the leader of the team, so things kind of went down. So here I am in 1979, and we're rebuilding all over again. . . ."

But when times get tough, McKenzie can stop time for the moment and think about a better day, like when he helped O. J. Simpson climb a mountain.

"I was in my second year and Joe DeLamielleure was in his first," remembers McKenzie about the golden 1973 season, "and I think the enthusiasm that we were bringing out of our respective schools into pro ball was catching. That just blended in with the experience that O. J. had. I know plenty of times a hole wouldn't be there, and he just made one of those unbelievable runs or a move, and you say, 'How did he see that guy?'

"Everybody wanted to see O. J. break Jim Brown's record and I tell you, I felt pretty proud about it. O. J. enjoyed running and I enjoyed blocking for the run, because of just personal satisfaction. An offensive lineman, that's the only thing he gets. And for me to say that I was a part of Simpson's 2,000-yard season, that's just one of the personal accomplishments you think about in football. It's not monetary or anything. Nobody can take that away from you."

BRAD VAN PELT

It was a life and death situation for Brad Van Pelt as he prepared to play the Detroit Lions this sober autumn day.

"I wanted to have an especially big game against Detroit, because I was playing out my option in New York and had very serious intentions of leaving the Giants and hooking on with Detroit," the Giants' All-Pro linebacker remembers. "So having a good game against them was going to help."

The inspiration was certainly there in more ways than one. Van Pelt was a native of Owosso, Michigan, who had grown up worshipping the Lions and playing his college ball at Michigan State. The game was to be televised back to his home state, as well.

The season was 1976, a rather grim one for him, he remembers.

"My dad passed away just the summer before," Van Pelt recalls, "and I more or less personally dedicated the year to him. That was the first season that I was going to be playing without him. I even had a black armband sewed on my jersey."

If one game could sum up Van Pelt's uncommon passions that year, it was the one against the Lions. Playing as he had never done before, or since, Van Pelt put on a true Hall of Fame performance that day: ten solo tackles, five assists, two interceptions, and two quarterback sacks.

Van Pelt's ferocity helped the Giants beat the Lions 24–10.

"I was really nervous before the game," says Van Pelt. "I can't remember the last time I had lost any sleep the night before a game. In college, I used to be up quite a bit with the nerves. You know, the band's playing in the morning, and I used to get shivers, chills down my back. But once you're a so-called professional, it's your job, and the nerves and the big excitement aren't supposed to be there anymore.

"But this Detroit game, it's the honest-to-God truth, I got about three or four hours of sleep the night before, and I was just like a little kid, I was so anxious to play. I really wanted to have a good game and I didn't know how to react. It was funny, because I was reliving my old college days."

If Van Pelt was nervous in college, it certainly didn't reflect in his heroic performances. He was a dynamic leader of the Michigan State defense for three solid years, performing nobly at the "monster" safety position. He was All-Big 10 three times, All-American twice, and the winner of the Maxwell Trophy, given each year by the Maxwell Club in Philadelphia to the best collegiate player in the country.

The Giants thought enough of Van Pelt to make him their first draft choice in 1973. His rookie season was clouded by a minor injury and an indecision by the coaching staff about where to play him. But after settling into his linebacker position in 1974, Van Pelt has been a powerful performer since.

Van Pelt really came into his own in the 1976 season when he won a spot in the Pro Bowl for the first time, as well as a place on the All-National Football Conference team. The Detroit game, of course, served as a spring-board that year for him.

"I guess my nervousness helped in that game," points out Van Pelt, "because I was just so pumped up the night before and all day. The adrenalin was flowing even before I stepped on the field. I just couldn't wait to go out there. Once you get on the field, the game is 80 to 90 percent mental. If you aren't ready to play, you aren't going to have a good game. Just looking back, I must have been going over everything in my mind, and that extra preparation helped me a lot."

Van Pelt made a noticeable impression right away, intercepting two of Greg Landry's passes within a four-minute period of the first quarter.

"I remember the Detroit papers played that up really big," Van Pelt says. "They were accusing Landry of throwing me the ball, because one of the passes was right at me."

When Landry wasn't throwing the ball at Van Pelt, he was being thrown himself by the sky-high New York linebacker.

"That year I ended up with three quarterback sacks," recalls Van Pelt, "and two of them were in that game."

Giants' coach John McVay called Van Pelt's perform-ance "inspired," and the inspiration seemed to rub off on the rest of the Giants, who recovered three Detroit fumbles and generally played their best game of an oth-erwise dismal season. They had lost nine straight games at one time, so the performance against the Lions was an especially sweet Sunday.

"I think that was our most satisfying victory," Van Pelt notes. "We beat the Washington Redskins earlier, but we caught them by surprise. The Seattle Seahawks were just another team with a record like ours. But the Lions were better than their record [6–6 entering the game] indicated. They had played some real good foot-ball that year, and we just went out and beat them."

With Van Pelt and his defensive teammates establishing the tone early, the Giants scored the game's first ten points. With 1:42 gone in the second quarter, Craig Morton threw an 11-yard touchdown pass to Ed Marshall to cap a five-play, 56-yard drive. The Giants made it 10–0 on Joe Danelo's 35-yard field goal less than three minutes later, following the recovery of a Detroit fumble.

A one-yard touchdown run by Detroit's Lawrence Gaines cut New York's lead to three points. But with less than a minute to go in the half, New York's Brad Cousino blocked a Detroit punt, and the Giants recovered near the Lions' goal line to set up another touchdown. Doug Kotar took a pitchout three yards around right end for the score and a 17–7 lead, which ultimately proved to be enough to carry the game.

Benny Ricardo connected on a 43-yard field goal just six seconds before the half for Detroit's final points. The Giants completed the scoring in the third quarter on a 35-yard touchdown pass from Morton to Marshall.

"The crowd was really alive that day," Van Pelt remembers. "Normally, you don't tend to hear them when you're playing. But I guess when you're winning like that, you get more of an opportunity to stand on the sidelines. When you're losing, I know as a defensive player I'm usually on the field most of the time. I can remember being aware of the crowd, so obviously we were winning and I was able to enjoy a little bit of the game from the sidelines."

After Van Pelt's biggest game, he still expressed a faint hope of joining the Lions at some future date, but the urgency seemed to be gone.

"Maybe I'd like to finish out my career with the Lions," he told the *New York Times*, "but that's someday. It's awfully hard to leave [New York] after four years here, with the frustrations and the records we've had."

Three years later, Van Pelt is still a revered member of the Giants and says of his winter dreams: "As long as the Giants still want me, I probably won't be in Detroit."

It's probable that Van Pelt may never again feel the emotions with another team that he did with the Giants, especially in that season of 1976 and that game against the Lions.

"My father had always handled my contract talks," Van Pelt says, "and I was waiting for him to fully recover from his first heart attack to help me with them that year. When he passed away, my first thought was to not leave home again. It really upset me to be away when something like that happened. Still, it was hard for me to concentrate on football, and then I decided to dedicate the season to my dad. At the end of the year, I was selected to the Pro Bowl, so I was super happy about that. It was my first trip. Plus I had by far my most memorable game in that year, against Detroit. So I look back on 1976 as the year and the game that I remember most."

ROCKY BLEIER

It was the kind of game that a running back dreams about. For Rocky Bleier, it was a glorious technicolor dream, with stereophonic sound.

"Someone in my caliber doesn't get that kind of a day very often," says the Pittsburgh Steelers' halfback. "And it was a game that was played back in Milwaukee, kind of in front of the hometown crowd."

Bleier was talking about his 163-yard rushing day against the Green Bay Packers in 1975, a game that was memorable in more ways than one for him.

"They were filming a documentary series called 'The Winners' and I was going to be part of it," Bleier recalls, "and it was a teammate of mine, Andy Russell, who raised the money for this specific documentary. They wanted to shoot some game footage, and Andy personally paid for all the arrangements."

Bleier chuckles.

"He carried my bags for me, made sure I wouldn't trip or hurt myself prior to the game, because he had $5,000 out of pocket invested in me."

It turned out to be a good investment for Russell, even though he had to buy his own footage back from National Football League Properties, Inc., which owns the rights to all professional films shot at NFL games.

"He ended up paying more than was necessary for the footage," Bleier points out, "but on the other hand, I did have a pretty good day—and his film crew got lots of good footage."

There was plenty of Bleier action to shoot that day. He carried the ball 35 times as the Steelers won 16–13.

"After that game, I took my hat off to all the runners who were the mainstays in football history, like your Jimmy Browns, Jimmy Taylors, Franco Harrises, and O. J. Simpsons, people who carry the ball 20 to 30 times a game," says Bleier, "because I realized firsthandedly what kind of a beating they had taken week in, week out, year in and year out. That was probably the worst beating I had taken physically in a game in my life. My longest gain of the day was something like 11 yards."

Quite frankly, Bleier hadn't had that many opportunities to carry the ball in his life before. Nothing had come easy for him as a pro, and the 1975 season marked the highpoint in a career that was heretofore clouded by a war injury in Vietnam.

Son of a bartender in Appleton, Wisconsin, Bleier won widespread recognition on the local high school football team and later played for Notre Dame's national champions in 1966. He was drafted by the Steelers after the 1967 season at Notre Dame, but didn't get a chance to play for them right away because of a higher priority draft from the U. S. Army. Bleier went grudgingly into the Vietnam War, vowing he would return to the pro football wars.

He did, but it took more than the two years he expected.

While on patrol one day, Bleier was hit by a North Vietnamese bullet in his left thigh, then further crippled when a grenade tore up his right foot. The wounds merited a discharge for Bleier, and he was told he would have trouble walking again, much less running.

But it didn't stop him from trying to make the Pittsburgh Steeler team once more. Bleier was fitted with a special shoe on his right foot, and wore sheer determination all over himself.

"I guess I did have some doubts deep inside," says Bleier. "When I first started to work out in the spring of 1970, boy, I knew I had a long way to go, that it was going to be a tough struggle, in that I didn't have the speed. But they put me on the injured reserve list, which bought another year for me. And then they put me on the taxi squad, which bought still another year. Then in 1972, I really had to prove my worth as a player, a contributer to the team, and I felt I did that year by playing on special teams."

Still, Bleier knew he would never be another Jimmy Brown.

"I looked at my situation at the time. I was the fifth or sixth running back on the team and I didn't play much. My only contribution was to the special teams, and I got depressed. I felt they weren't using me, they didn't have confidence in me. I didn't want to be a special teams player all my life. I thought maybe I should retire."

A bad hamstring pull at the start of his comeback in 1971 had complicated matters.

"I had been out of action for three weeks. I missed the first two exhibition games that year. We were playing Green Bay in a preseason game, and I just went along with the team. I remember I went home to see the folks on that trip and really did some soul-searching. I asked myself: What are my options? I'm not 100 percent healed. If I wait until it heals, I might not make the team because time's running out. But if I go back and wrap up the leg and hope for the best at least I have a chance of making the team, if I don't pull it again."

Bleier talked to a family friend who happened to be a priest. Together they decided that Bleier should give football one more try.

"When I was activated later on," remembers Bleier,

"I pulled that hamstring again during the season. But at least I didn't miss another year."

By 1974, Bleier had a chance to start in a game. And by 1975, he had a chance to star.

"We ran basically very few plays that day," Bleier recalls of his big game against Green Bay. "It was kind of a combination of plays that we ran, and several times I can remember one of their outside linebackers was so confused on what we were doing, he didn't know whether we were passing or what his coverage was. One play we would run inside of him, another play we would run outside of him, and I can remember turning a corner one time and he was backpedaling and looking over his shoulder trying to decipher where he was to go.

"And it was a game that had a lot of things in it. For one, I was doing a lot of running. I had some passes, too. I fumbled in the game. We had the ball once driving down into Green Bay territory, getting down close, and I think the score was 7–3 at the time in favor of Green Bay. I had the ball up the middle and I ran ... I fumbled, it wasn't a clean handoff. I got hit by Mike McCoy. Of course Mike and I had played together in college. And when he hit me and I fumbled, he basically bear-hugged me so I couldn't get the ball, and as we were falling down, all he was saying was: 'Thank you, Rocky; thank you, Rocky; thank you, Rocky.' "

That was about all the Packers could thank Bleier for that afternoon. Otherwise, he was nearly perfect, thanks to a couple of plays that were numerically listed as "84."

"We had two plays that were basically running plays that were really working fairly well that day," recalls Bleier. "One was called the '84 Trap,' which is a halfback, or the far back, carrying into the four hole, on the right side. It was a trap play. We were trapping the defensive end. So what happens is the end releases down to the middle linebacker, the tackle comes down on the defensive tackle, the guard pulls and traps the defensive end, and the fullback comes up and seals or kicks out the linebacker that was over the tight end.

"Now the companion play to that is called the '84 Special.' Everything basically at the point of attack is the same, except now the fullback blocks the defensive end down and the guard then goes around and takes the outside linebacker. The idea is if you have a defensive end, you start trapping him, and then all of a sudden if he starts to close the trap and you can't get a good trapping angle on him, then you just call the 'Special.' Since the defensive end is coming down at an angle, the fullback just goes in and whams him and takes him down, and the guard pulls up around the fullback's block and picks up the linebacker. And then you take it outside. One's an inside play and one's an outside play, so it kind of confuses because at the initial snap, everything's the same with the first two steps."

The victory was one of the rungs by which the Steelers climbed to the top of the NFL. Later they won the Super Bowl with Rocky playing a significant role, another moment in his pro career that proved pure magic for him.

"I was super high and emotional for that game," remembers Bleier. "The Steelers had never gotten to the Super Bowl before, and I can plainly remember standing in that runway before being introduced and thinking about all the great teams that had played before us in the Super Bowls . . . and just thinking that here was a little kid from Appleton, Wisconsin, who is able to participate in one as a starting running back."

But it was the Green Bay game earlier in the season that gave Bleier a special sense of individual accomplishment.

"It was a special day for me," Bleier says, "because it made me feel that I had the capability of gaining 100-plus yards in a game. It made me feel I had the ability to be a starting back. I knew then that I could contribute and be worthwhile."

DOUG WILLIAMS

As far as Doug Williams is concerned, the pass is prologue. But when there is a choice between passing and winning, Doug will pass on the former and take the latter.

Such a situation came up once in Tokyo, Japan, he remembers, when his Grambling football team was eight yards away from a touchdown in the late stages of a close game with Temple.

"I had already thrown 38 touchdown passes that season, and if I could have thrown one more, I would have tied Dennis Shaw's record for the most ever [at a Division I school]," says Williams. "We called time out and I went over to coach [Eddie] Robinson to discuss the play that we were going to call, and he wanted a pass play. And I looked at him and said, 'No.' He asked me what that meant, no. I told him everyone in the ballpark was waiting on a pass. So he said, 'What do you think?' And I told him a 37-Sweep, which was a sweep to the right side. And he said, 'Okay.' "

So Williams, who had already thrown three touchdown passes in the game, sidestepped a chance to get into the record books, putting personal interests aside for a far more noble cause.

"We called a sweep and everybody in the ballpark backed up," says Williams. "I think Temple had about two guys rushing, because everybody was looking for the pass. And our guy just went in untouched. It was the greatest thrill of my life."

Floyd Womack was the player who ran the ball over for the Grambling touchdown, and it couldn't have come at a more appropriate time. It happened with 30 seconds left and provided the Tigers with a dramatic 35–32 victory.

Williams, now a successful quarterback in the National Football League with the Tampa Bay Buccaneers, is apt to remember that game even more, considering it was his last as a collegian, at the end of the 1977 season.

"It was sort of a revenge game, too," says Williams, "because we had lost to Temple the year before in Philadelphia, 31–30, in the last 33 seconds. And that's what made it so great. Because the thing that they did to us, we came back and did to them. I remember, the Temple quarterback and I had a few words, but it was more of a competitive thing, because he had had a great game against us in Philadelphia the year before. He threw a last-second touchdown pass to beat us. So it was just a great feeling to come back like we did in that game in Tokyo and let them know that we could do the same thing."

That element of pride sticks out on Williams like a sore-thumbed quarterback. Ever since he knew he could throw a football faster and farther than most people, he wanted to go to Grambling. And after becoming Grambling's greatest quarterback, he wanted professional acceptance. There was more to it than being just a great NFL quarterback, of course. There was the matter of his skin color. Blacks are not supposed to be quarterbacks, so they say. But Williams says differently:

"Blacks are not supposed to be quarterbacks because they don't give blacks a chance to be quarterbacks."

There is no rancor in Williams's voice, just quiet determination.

"I feel if you're given a chance, anybody can be what they want to be," he says softly.

From an early age, Williams wanted to be a quarterback. Growing up in a small factory town called Zachary, Louisiana, he tuned up his arm by throwing stones. "When I was a kid," he remembers, "I was always picking up stones and throwing them at mailboxes, stop signs, and freight trains. I may even have broken a few windows." He threw footballs as well as anyone had ever seen in Zachary, too, and his high school career earned him some scholarship offers. He took the one to Grambling because he had been thinking about that school since he was seven years old. "It was a dream come true," Williams says.

Williams was a dream come true for Grambling, too. The school often referred to as "the Notre Dame of black football" recorded a 35–5 record under this gifted player. Among his many achievements at the Louisiana school, Williams threw for an NCAA all-division record of 93 touchdowns and accounted for 96, another standard. His career total passing yardage of 8,411 is second in NCAA all-division history, and he also holds Division I marks for yards per completion in a season (18.2) and yards per attempt in a season (9.34), both set in 1977, and an all-division career record for 17.4 yards per completion. Uniquely, Williams threw a touchdown pass in every game but one during his glittering Grambling career.

During his last year, when Williams compiled 38 touchdown passes and 3,286 yards, he and the rest of the people at Grambling figured he had a good chance to win the Heisman Trophy, given each year to the best college football player in the country. But he finished a disappointing fourth.

"I'm not saying I should have won the Heisman,"

says Williams, "but if you find any quarterback who had my stats and didn't, let me know."

Williams remembers that he found out about the Heisman results while the Grambling team was training in Tokyo for the Temple game. "Even though I finished fourth," he recalls, "I wasn't even invited to the Heisman dinner.

"Coach Robinson knew about it, but he didn't want to tell me right away for fear of upsetting me. He thought if I found out I didn't win the Heisman, I would have been too upset to play. But when I found out during the week, I told him, 'Hey, you don't have to worry about me because I didn't win it. A lot of people know why they win it (image, politics) and we're not going to worry about it.' But what happened after the Temple game really made me feel good. I can remember coming into the dressing room and coach Robinson told me and the rest of the guys that he didn't care what anybody said, or whatever anyone did, but we had our own Heisman Trophy winner in the room. I thought he paid me a great compliment. . . ."

Williams looked every bit the Heisman Trophy winner in that 1977 contest against Temple, especially in the game's closing minutes when Grambling trailed by four points with about three minutes left. The ball rested on Grambling's own 15-yard line, the potential winning score 85 long yards away.

"All the players on the team looked a bit shell-shocked," recalls Williams. "They were scared . . . everything was just quiet. But everybody seemed to believe in me. One big lineman, I remember, was looking up at the clock, telling me the time that was left. The first two plays we called were draw plays, and on those two plays we must have come up with about 40 yards. We were in great field position.

"The next one was a quick pitchout to Robert Woods and we got about five or six yards; the next one was a ten-yard out to Carlos Pennywell. You know, we really started to move the ball at this point."

Then the Grambling offense slowed down for a while.

"We just stalled," Williams remembers, "three downs, two incomplete passes, and one run. Now it was something like fourth-and-nine, on about the Temple 18."

It was an obvious passing stuation, and Grambling's pass master expected to do exactly that, except that all of Williams's receivers were covered. "I had to scramble," he says. Scramble he did for a first down, to the Temple eight-yard line, setting the stage for Womack's winning touchdown run.

Grambling, a virtual goodwill ambassador for collegiate sports, had been the first American college football team to play in Japan, starting that tradition the year before in a game with Morgan State. So this victory made it two in a row for the Tigers in the Far East, establishing them as kind of a hometown favorite. The size of the crowd reflected Grambling's popularity.

"The stadium was packed when we were there," says Williams. "They must have had about 55,000 people, some of them sitting in the aisles. That made it even more exciting. And then after the game, I had to run to the bus, because the little Japanese kids were going to tackle me to sign autographs. I guess there were hundreds of kids waiting for us outside the stadium after that game."

If the Japanese were not as sophisticated as American fans, they at least knew a good football player when they saw one. While Grambling's fine quarterback was leading the team down the field on several occasions, the scoreboard flashed the sign: "Go, Williams, Go!"

"I missed it," said Williams, "but a teammate told me after the game: 'You should have seen the scoreboard.' I guess I was too busy."

What plays were working for Williams that day?

"We were throwing on just about everything. We had Woods, an outstanding track man who was a world-class runner. I threw a lot of short passes to him, and Pennywell caught a 94-yarder in that game, a touch-down pass. I'll never forget that one, it was on a post pattern."

Williams called his own plays and admittedly "liked to throw the football." But he's glad he refrained from throwing it when the game was on the line at the end.

"I'm glad I was man enough to realize that tying the [passing] record didn't mean anything," Williams says. "I wanted to win, and I decided that a running play would be best in that situation."

Williams continued rolling in the pros, after being drafted by Tampa Bay. He was the unanimous choice as the all-NFL rookie quarterback in 1978, after passing for 1,170 yards and seven touchdowns in eight games and parts of two others. In the games he finished, the Bucs were 4–4. Injuries prevented him from completing his two other starts.

In his second season, Williams became one of the most respected quarterbacks in the league while leading the expansion team to its first winning record. Along the way, he has won praise from Johnny Unitas, one of the great all-time quarterbacks, who says: "Williams has the arm and quickness to be a great one, and his tremendous wrist action makes him hard to sack."

Says Tampa Bay coach John McKay: "Williams has more natural ability than any quarterback I've ever seen. I always thought Norm Van Brocklin had the strongest arm I'd ever seen, but now I'm changing my mind. I saw Doug hit Morris Owens with a 60-yard bomb in practice that he threw with just a flick of the wrist. All Doug needs to do is play to become possibly the best quarterback in football."

Williams feels that McKay showed a good deal of courage in selecting him on the first round, ignoring the prevailing attitude toward black quarterbacks and the possibility of backlash should he have failed.

"Sixteen other clubs had a chance to draft me before coach McKay did," says Williams. "But he did, not worrying about that black quarterback thing, or whatever they call it. He had the guts to give me a chance to play. There's no color barrier here. He's trying to put together a team and he doesn't care if you're black, white, or blue."

Alluding to possible prejudice in the NFL, McKay said on the day of the draft: "All things being equal, Doug Williams would have been picked much earlier otherwise. We're not dummies; we know why he wasn't."

Since then, Williams has become virtually color blind.

"All I think about is being one of the best quarterbacks in the league," Williams says. "I'm not thinking in terms of black or white."

McKay certainly sees the possibilities.

"I would think if there is anything like a franchise, whatever that is, I guess he'd be that," says the Tampa Bay coach.

JIM ZORN

Jim Zorn's "Super Sunday" happened on a Monday night. A "Miracle Monday," as some writers have called it.

The Seattle Seahawks were in Atlanta to play their first-ever game on the Monday night television broadcast, and the left-handed quarterback was definitely right for the occasion. The date was October 29, 1979.

"You feel as if the whole world is watching," says Zorn, clearly one of the rising young stars in the National Football League. "When you make a mistake, a lot of people know about it."

Zorn didn't make many mistakes that night, but he did make a national TV audience sit up and take notice of his highly creative performance. Before Zorn's Seahawks had put away a wild 31–28 victory, there was enough flash and dash to last for a whole season of Monday night telecasts.

Throwing all football logic to the sidelines, the Seahawks took enough chances to make a riverboat gambler cash in his chips, like:

● A quarterback draw on fourth-and-five at the Atlanta 34 that Zorn took in for his team's first touchdown.

● A fake field goal on a fourth-and-five at the Atlanta 37 that Zorn turned into a 20-yard gain with a pass to kicker Efren Herrera.

● A brash fake punt by Herman Weaver on a fourth-and-12 from the Seattle 32 that failed when Weaver completed a pass that was three yards short.

● A run by Dan Doornink on a fourth-and-one at the Atlanta 46 that netted 13 yards and allowed Seattle to retain possession with six minutes left.

Add a gorgeous onside kick by Herrera at the most unexpected moment, and you get the picture. The Seahawks got away with murder in a city that had just been cited as the homicide capital of the nation.

"We did a lot of different things," says Zorn. "It was fun."

Zorn has had better games statistically (witness his 24-of-33 passing day for 384 yards and four touchdowns against the New Orleans Saints later in the season), but fat individual numbers don't necessarily make him high.

"It is more important for me," he says, "for the team to do well, for the plays to work, and of course to win."

In this respect, one of the NFL's newest franchises and one of its youngest teams has steadily improved, thanks to Zorn, who reflects the seemingly swaggering attitude of the Seahawks. Not that they don't care, just that they're "loose," according to one player. "We're a young, enthusiastic team building more confidence day by day," says receiver Steve Largent, Zorn's favorite target.

About his development as a quarterback, Zorn says: "It's been a pleasant surprise for me, but I still have a lot to learn. As far as maturity goes, I know more than I ever have in the past. The problem comes when I do not know a situation and respond to it properly. If you give me a test on paper, I could do it in a second. If there is a problem, it's when I walk up to the line of scrimmage. It takes experience and I'm trying to get it as fast as I can. Sometimes I pick things up and sometimes I don't."

Zorn was a gifted athlete at Cal Poly Pomona, where he led the small colleges in total offense in 1973, but ironically was ignored by everyone in the 1975 NFL draft. He signed as a walk-on with the Dallas Cowboys, but was cut. He finally found a job with Seattle, just as the Seahawks were entering the league in 1976. Zorn wasted little time winning the no. 1 quarterback job and making a name for himself. In the Seahawks' very first exhibition game, Zorn came off the bench and displayed some high-powered scoring proficiency. He went on to become the National Conference's offensive rookie of the year, throwing for 2,571 yards and 12 touchdowns. By 1978 he was the hottest thing going in the NFL, amassing 3,283 yards in the air with 248 passes completed in 443 attempts, a whopping 56 percent. After Zorn's phenomenal day against New Orleans in 1979, during which he became only the third quarterback in NFL history to pass for 10,000 yards in his first four seasons, Saints' quarterback Archie Manning described him as "fantastic."

Zorn would modestly disagree with that assessment.

"Some days are better than others," says Zorn, who has also had his off-days in a roller-coaster career. In a 24–0 loss to the Los Angeles Rams in 1979, the proud, young Seahawks were held to a minus-seven yards on offense, an NFL record in futility.

"I promised myself I wouldn't forget that Ram game —and I haven't," Zorn says. "There are lots of things to learn from a game like that. We were prepared, but we just didn't execute."

That was not the case, however, when Seattle played Atlanta in that memorable Monday night game. In that contest, Zorn says he faced one of the NFL's best blitzing teams.

"They're known for their blitz," Zorn says of the Falcons, "and I wasn't particularly looking forward to it. The Houston blitz was tough in an earlier game that season. But this one was tougher. They had as many as nine men on the line at times."

The prospect of facing that blitz before the national TV cameras, Zorn says, made him "nervous" at first, "but then I got used to it."

Meanwhile, the Falcons were trying to get used to the crazy-quilt Seattle style.

"I don't really have any special style," says Zorn. "Just whatever works for us. We try a lot of different things."

After taking a 14–0 lead in the game's first 16 minutes, the Falcons saw a lot of different faces under Zorn's silvery Seattle helmet.

First came Zorn's quarterback draw from the Falcon 34. With Atlanta's defenders decoyed to the sidelines by potential receivers, Zorn slid through a gaping hole in the Falcon line and went in practically untouched. With Herrera's kick, the Atlanta lead was cut to 14–7 with 9:25 remaining in the half.

Explaining that unexpected play, Seahawks' offensive coordinator Jerry Rhome told Don Fair of the *Seattle Post Intelligencer:* "Jim made all the right reads. They were coming with everybody, and we caught them in man-to-man coverage, the receivers taking the secondary people wide. It was read right and we blocked it right. Jim reads his linemen's blocks and reacts accordingly. Hey, Atlanta blitzed more tonight that it has all year. They blitzed nearly every down in the last half. If you live by the sword, you die by it. They can make big plays on you, but if you catch them right, you get big ones, too."

On their next possession, the Seahawks were still defying convention a bit. Four yards away from a touchdown, in a situation that would normally dictate an inside power play, Zorn went over—not inside—the Atlanta line with a TD pass to Sherman Smith. The Seahawks had taken practically no time at all to score this time, getting into the end zone on a sweet, six-play drive after Tony Green's fine punt return set them up in good field position at the Atlanta 38.

So now with the score tied at 14–14, it was time for the surging Seahawks to drive a long kick down the Falcons' collective throat and leave the rest to the defense, right?

Wrong.

Now it was time for Herrera to pull an onside kick and cross your fingers.

The ruse worked. Atlanta fumbled conveniently, allowing Keith "Big Play" Simpson to recover for Seattle at the Falcon 42. Three plays later, the Seahawks were on the 37 and lined up in field goal formation for the strong-footed Herrera.

The Falcons were braced for a field goal attempt, but it turned out that the Seahawks were only kidding this time. Instead of Herrera kicking, it was Herrera catching. Zorn kept the ball and threw it to the kicker, who scrambled out of the backfield and raced through the stunned Falcons for a 20-yard gain and a first down at the 17.

"You don't call these plays every day," says Zorn, "but we don't call them gambles. Unusual, maybe, but not gambles. We work on them seriously in practice. We don't laugh about it, but everybody enjoys it. We just let it all out that game."

About those oddball plays, Seattle coach Jack Patera told reporters: "I felt comfortable with the fake field goal. Fourth and five with the quarterback running is touchy . . . not a sure thing, but there is something about the nature of our team that makes it worth gambling. We have people who can do these things. Herrera is a good kicker and a good receiver."

Had Herrera ever done this in a game before? Why, no, said Patera, "but he catches the ball real well in practice."

The way things were going for Seattle, everything was

working—even the conventional things. Three running plays later, the Seahawks scored again, on a relatively unassuming eight-yard blast by Dan Doornink through a plethora of tacklers.

Now it was 21–14 in favor of the Seahawks, and everyone in Atlanta Stadium could see the way things were going.

But no one could envision what would happen thereafter.

After taking a 24–14 lead on Herrera's 24-yard field goal at 8:14 of the third period, the Seahawks continued to do zany things—like faking a punt on fourth down and letting Weaver throw a pass. The pass by the kicker was completed for nine yards, but it fell short of the first down and allowed Atlanta to take over on the Seattle 41. The Falcons drove to the Seattle six-yard line but couldn't take advantage of the opportunity as Tim Mazzetto missed a relatively easy field goal.

In the fourth quarter, the Seahawks made things even more interesting by fumbling deep in their own territory, and the Falcons took-advantage of it with a subsequent 17-yard touchdown pass from Steve Bartkowski to Billy Ryckman with 10:03 left. But Seattle later appeared to have the game wrapped up when a 26-yard TD run by Doornink with 1:51 to go gave them a 31–21 lead.

(Earlier, it was this same Doornink who had kept a Seattle drive going with a 13-yard run on a fourth-and-one from the Atlanta 46, a situation that might have called for a punt in conservative circles. However, this drive was later stalled when the Seahawks fumbled and the Falcons recovered at their 26.)

So Zorn went to the sidelines with that 10-point lead and a world of unshakable faith.

"It feels good to win," he told Patera.

"Don't say that—yet," said the Seattle coach.

It turned out that Patera's fears were well-founded, as the Falcons rushed back behind Bartkowski's expert direction. The Atlanta quarterback completed five straight passes and capped a 66-yard drive with a 20-yard strike to Ryckman that cut Seattle's lead to 31–28 with 51 seconds remaining.

Was Zorn jittery at this point? Well, not really.

"My thoughts were, it's either overtime or we're behind. But if they had scored again, there's nothing we could have done. I was only worried about doing my job."

But the Falcons didn't give Zorn that chance. Taking a page from Seattle's book, they made an onside kick and recovered it, then marched down to the Seahawk 13-yard line. The Falcon-oriented crowd of 52,566 was screaming for a miracle now, and they got one—but it was from the wrong side. As Bartkowski fired into the end zone, Seattle's Dave Brown went up and made a miraculous interception with 35 seconds remaining, thus preserving an electrifying victory for the Seahawks. As Patera was to say later, "The turning point wasn't the gambles we made. The turning point was Dave Brown's interception."

And Zorn would have to second that motion.

"Bartkowski did a super job coming back the way he did," he says. "But Dave Brown and the rest of the guys hung in there and got the key play. That's what really won it for us."

DARYLE LAMONICA

Outside of a blind-side tackle by a churlish defensive end, nothing hurts a quarterback more than to have a touchdown pass called back on a penalty. And when it happens to be a particularly artistic toss with the game on the line in the final minutes, well, that hurts even more.

It happened to Oakland's Daryle Lamonica in the notorious and frenetic "Heidi Game" of 1968 against the New York Jets.

"I had Charley Smith coming out of the backfield," Lamonica remembers. "We had less than two minutes left in the game. It was a third-and-five situation, I think, and I hit him on like a 65-yard or 70-yard touchdown pass that was called back because somebody was in motion."

New York defensive back Johnny Sample approached Lamonica at this point with a smile and said, "Nice play, Daryle, but too bad it didn't count. Maybe you'll do better next year."

The needle hurt as much as the penalty. Says Lamonica:

"I told him, 'The game's not over with yet, John.

There's still a lot of time to go.' And he laughed and said, 'No way.' "

Losing 32–29, the Raiders were forced to punt. But the defense held and Lamonica got a second chance. This time, nobody made mistakes and Lamonica threw a 43-yard touchdown pass to Smith with 42 seconds left in the game for a 36–32 Oakland lead. And not long thereafter, Preston Ridlehuber recovered a Jets fumble on the kickoff and scored yet another Oakland touchdown.

The final score: Oakland 43, New York 32.

"That game probably gave me more personal satisfaction than any other game, knowing that we never did quit," says Lamonica. "From a quarterback's standpoint, it was a wonderful game . . . you know, coming back to beat the Jets and being able to tell them after the game: I told you there was a lot of time left."

The Raiders had made similar magic against the Jets earlier, [1970], winning on a last-second touchdown play. But for Lamonica, it wasn't nearly as artistic as the "Heidi Game."

"That earlier game," says Lamonica, "was just luck. The clock ran out as the ball was in the air and Warren Wells just happened to catch it. But in the Heidi Game, we worked on this particular pass play with Smith all week, and we knew that if we caught the right defense, it would work."

Ironically, this storybook ending to a spectacular football game was shut off to television viewers in most of the nation. NBC officials, in an error of judgment they would long regret, opted to go with the children's movie, "Heidi," precisely at the regularly programmed time of 7 p.m., EST, thus cutting off the game's last minute to viewers in the Midwest, South, and East.

"I know it blew a lot of circuits in New York," Lamonica remembers. "Of course we didn't know anything about it at the time. We were just trying to win a football game."

The Jets had gone ahead 32–29 on Jim Turner's field goal, with 1:05 left and television viewers saw the Raiders return the kickoff and run one play. Then NBC threw a switch in New York to start "Heidi" flowing from East to West, and football fans began throwing tantrums. The inappropriate move by NBC triggered such a deluge of phone calls to headquarters in New York that an operator said the fuses in the switchboard actually blew out. Many irate fans who couldn't get through to NBC started calling the police department, newspapers, and radio stations, in fact anyone who would listen to their complaints in New York. The New York Telephone Co. was also harrassed by callers who wanted to know why they couldn't reach NBC.

Julian Goodman, president of the television network at the time, admitted that NBC fumbled the ball but not intentionally. "It was a forgivable error committed by human beings who were concerned about the children expecting to see 'Heidi' at 7 p.m. I missed the end of the game as much as anyone else."

This error was later compounded when NBC ran the final score of the game in a streamer across the bottom of the screen during the showing of "Heidi." The streamer came at a particular touching moment in the movie, as Heidi's paralytic cousin Klara tried to walk, and this insensitive intrusion sparked indignation in the "Heidi" fans.

The New York Daily News, among others, didn't help stir up any sympathy for the network, either, with this headline the next day: "Jets 32, Raiders, 29, Heidi 14."

Meanwhile, the game had a different kind of impact on the Raiders.

"It just proved to myself as well as my teammates that if we'd hang in there, we could make things happen," says Lamonica. "We fought adversity, had that one touchdown pass called back, and still never gave up. And that year we went on to win our division."

The "Heidi Game" ranks right up there with some of

the National Football League's most memorable contests, and not only because of NBC's short circuit. It matched two of the game's finest passers in Lamonica and New York's Joe Namath and was rife with theatrical moments.

"Joe Willie and I had another one of our big battles," recalls Lamonica. "I always enjoyed playing against Joe, because we both liked to put the ball in the air and we made the game exciting."

Lamonica threw four touchdown passes this day, two of them in the first half to help the Raiders establish a 14–12 lead at intermission. Jim Turner kicked two field goals and Namath ran the ball over from the one for the Jets' first-half points.

The Jets took a 19–14 lead after intermission on a four-yard touchdown run by Bill Mathis, only to see Oakland move in front again, 22–19, on a three-yard TD dash by Smith and a two-point conversion. Namath then completed a 50-yard touchdown pass play to Don Maynard to give the Jets the lead at 26–22. That didn't last long, as Lamonica hooked up on a 22-yard touchdown pass with Fred Biletnikoff. Now the Raiders led once more, 29–26.

But it was far from over.

Namath quickly moved the Jets into field-goal range, and Turner kicked a 12-yarder to tie the game at 29–29. Turner later kicked another from 26 yards to put the Jets into a 32–29 lead.

Then it was over—as far as NBC was concerned. But not for the Raiders, who came winging back on Lamonica's arm to pull out one of the most dramatic games in NFL history.

It was a typical Lamonica performance, indicative of his highly creative style, which some thought occasionally leaned toward flamboyancy.

"Just by nature, I'm not a conservative individual," Lamonica says, "and I believed that by being a quarterback, you should make things happen. I think anytime you get conservative on a football field, you have trouble. My philosophy was, once you get two touchdowns up on your opponent, that's the time to go after them. If you make a mistake then, it won't cost you nearly as much than if it was a tight ballgame. You don't get to the point where you're reckless and you gamble foolishly, but you take advantage of situations."

Lamonica didn't have the opportunity to express himself as he would have liked while playing for Notre Dame and Joe Kuharich's sober, conservative system in the early 1960s.

"I was, without a doubt, disappointed in my years at Notre Dame," says Lamonica, who was only used sporadically by Kuharich, the only losing coach in Notre Dame history. "Kuharich never liked to use audibles. He thought the play you called in the huddle should go regardless of the defense. And, you know, I found myself with a first and ten on the 20-yard line getting goal-line defenses. It was frustrating, to say the least."

But Lamonica, only son of a Fresno, California, rancher, later was able to express himself fully when he was invited to the 1962 East-West Shrine Game. There, unencumbered, he passed for a record 349 yards with 20 completions in 28 attempts and was voted the game's Most Valuable Player.

"I found out I really had a lot of ability," Lamonica says, "and I just knew I could play in the pros if I got the opportunity and could stay healthy."

Lamonica was drafted by the Buffalo Bills of the old American Football League and had to fight his way through a forest of quarterbacks to stick with the team, behind no. 1 man Jack Kemp.

"I remember when I first started out in the pros, I felt if I could just make two years, I'd be lucky. And then when I got to two, I was shooting for three. Then I thought about five years and my pension. After that, it was one year at a time. I didn't live in fear of injury, but I knew that on any given play, my career could be ended. And fortunately for me, it didn't happen."

Lamonica finally walked away from football under his own power in 1975 after 13 years and three teams. During that period he got a lot done, establishing a raft of Oakland passing records and leading the Raiders to their first Super Bowl appearance, in 1967.

Before joining Oakland and raising his profile considerably, the 6-foot-3, 220-pound Lamonica was an eager and attentive apprentice under the care of Lou Saban at Buffalo. Lamonica learned quickly and even was called upon to pull out some games for the often-erratic Kemp in 1964, when the Bills won the AFL championship.

"I think I made it relatively quick in the pros," Lamonica tells you. "I felt like a starter in Buffalo, as soon as I relieved Jack Kemp and pulled out some games, and helped us win four straight division championships. So I felt I had a chance to show some of my talent, and of course naturally being young and aggressive, it gave me a chance to learn. No quarterback, and that includes Joe Namath, has ever stepped in and won right off the bat. It took him four years before he could really break in."

In 1966, however, Lamonica was still sitting on the bench for the most part and craving more action. He got it when the Bills traded him to Oakland after that season.

"I was very excited about the trade," Lamonica says, "but, at the same time, hurt from the standpoint that the Bills had given up on me. It's funny, but I had talked to Ralph Wilson, Jr., the owner of the Bills, just the night before. And he had said the team was really looking forward to me coming back and helping Buffalo win another championship. So I was excited about that, but in eight hours I was traded. So it was sort of a shock."

But it was also an opportunity for Lamonica to get back on the West Coast, where he was born.

"So I said, all-in-all, maybe that was my break, and I analyzed it as such, and tried just to capitalize on the situation."

Lamonica found the Oakland system a bit more complex than the one in Buffalo. But he worked hard at mastering it—and he had a lot of help.

"From the day I was traded, I spent an awful lot of time meeting with coach John Rauch. We spent hours— I can't even tell you how many hours we spent—going over the system. And I think a big key, from my early success with the Raiders, was my roommate, a fellow by the name of Cotton Davidson. He was a quarterback and a competitor, but he helped me. I don't know how many nights I kept him awake asking him questions. And he saved me probably more bumps and bruises than anyone. He would say, 'Daryle, don't do that. I can tell you from past experience, you do that and you're going to get knocked on your butt.' And he'd tell me what formations to use for certain situations."

Obviously Lamonica was a fast learner. In no time at all, actually his first season in Oakland, he led the Raiders to the AFL championship and was named the league's Player of the Year. Lifted by Lamonica's award-winning arm, the Raiders became the terrors of the league through the late 1960s and early 1970s.

"At that time, I had two great receivers in Warren Wells and Fred Biletnikoff, and it was kind of a pleasure to be able to throw to individuals like that," says Lamonica. "Of course it was my job to put the ball in the air, but I did try to go with a balanced attack. I wanted our opposition to fear the run as well as the pass. We never really had a breakaway runner, like a Walter Payton or O. J. Simpson who could go 80, 90 yards and bust the game wide open. So we did it a lot of times with the pass. But our running game was effective enough where they had to respect the big backs."

Along with the so-called "Heidi Game," some of Lamonica's other high-powered performances included six-touchdown passing days against both the Buffalo Bills and Los Angeles Rams.

Lamonica is apt to remember the one against the Bills, especially since he missed a record-tying seventh TD pass just a couple of yards from the goal line when receiver Drew Buie inadvertently stepped out of bounds. All of these touchdown passes, mind you, came before the first half. Says Lamonica:

"I can recall in the huddle on that particular play, Drew said, 'I got him deep.' And I said, 'You got it.' I laid it out for him and he caught it, but then stepped out of bounds. When he came back to the huddle, he just said, 'I just lost where the flight of the ball was. I had it all the way.' "

Lamonica had a ball while in Oakland from 1967 through 1974, passing for 16,655 yards and 148 touchdowns. He also wound up throwing a club-record 2,248 passes in those years, completing 1,138 of them, a 50.6 percentage. Lamonica's greatest statistical season in Oakland came in 1969, when he passed for 3,302 yards and 34 TDs.

In the final year of his career, he jumped to the short-lived World Football League in 1975, where he played in only one game for the Southern California Sun before a hernia put him on the sidelines. He then retired.

"I could have probably played three or four more years, if I'd wanted to," Lamonica says. "But I got out because I wanted to get out. I had already had a double hernia operation, and I didn't want to go under the knife again. I just felt that I had contributed and done the things I wanted to in the game, and I got out while I still had my health. I walked away from the game before I felt I was just hanging on."

Besides, there were other things Lamonica wanted to do.

"I dabble in real estate now," says Lamonica. "I'm kind of self-employed, doing my own investing."

Lamonica has found the business world "no different from a football game."

"You go through your rookie year and get kicked around a little bit," he says. "Then you trust a few people, and you find out that they take advantage of you in little ways. But you serve your apprenticeship, just like I did on the Bills, until you discover you're ready for it."

If Lamonica throws as much effort into his business interests as he did into football, he should be yards ahead of the competition.

BOB THOMAS

This was a game Bob Thomas would have liked to forget . . . until the last eight seconds of overtime. Then it turned out to be a game he will always remember.

His Chicago Bears overcame all kinds of adversity, including some of the worst football weather this side of Green Bay and a bundle of mistakes, to defeat the die-hard New York Giants 12–9 on the last day of the regular 1977 National Football League season.

The result not only saved face for a mistake-prone Chicago team but put the Bears in the NFL playoffs for the first time in 14 years. Of course Bob Thomas will remember it especially, since he kicked the winning field goal.

"I remember with the clock ticking down, [coach] Jack Pardee didn't even have Bob Avellini throw the ball out of bounds," Thomas recalls. "We didn't have any timeouts left. He just said, 'Field goal team,' and we ran on the field with no huddle or anything. We just ran up, set up the field goal . . . snap came back . . . I don't think I stopped running from the time I got off the sidelines to the time I kicked the ball and ran into the locker room. My prayer must have worked."

Thomas could also have been praying not to fall on

the seat of his pants while attempting the dramatic kick. Just about everything else had befallen him and his team prior to the golden moment.

"It was the worst weather I ever played in," Thomas remembers. "Paul Hornung on the air described it as the worst possible conditions for anybody, especially kickers because it was so slippery out there. There was a freezing rain, then there was snow and there was slush, and it just kept coming down. It was like playing on a hockey rink. And it was bitterly cold because it was damp."

It certainly didn't look like it was going to be that kind of a day when the Bears arrived 24 hours before for a brief loosening-up drill at Giants Stadium in East Rutherford, N.J.

"We got there for practice on a Saturday," Thomas recalls, "and it was just beautiful. It was 55 or 60 degrees and sunny. We went through our kicking drill, and I remember thinking about what a great place this was going to be to kick in."

But later they heard the weather report for Sunday.

"Coach Pardee started to express concern about what type of cleats we were going to wear, because he said there was a chance of some snow flurries and some sleety type of rain. By the time we got on the field for Sunday's game, it was just awful."

The Bears would have preferred to play such an important game under better conditions, of course. They needed nothing less than a victory to get to the playoffs. Even a tie would have sent the Washington Redskins instead as the wild card entry in the National Conference.

"The field got covered quickly with this ice," Thomas recalls, and it made it very tough to kick in, to run on, to do anything on. . . ."

The Bears scored first on a Thomas field goal, but then their problems began.

"Everything that could possibly go wrong on a field did that afternoon. I missed a field goal . . . hit the upright with one, as I slipped. We had a missed blocking assignment on an extra point, and the guy shot right in and blocked it. We tried another field goal, and because of the weather conditions, the holder bobbled the ball. I never got to kick it. The holder tried to throw a pass to one of the wingbacks, which fell incomplete."

Thomas wasn't the only one having trouble for the Bears. Walter Payton, their leading rusher, fumbled the ball three times—twice on one play. The other Bears fumbled five times more. Payton, incidentally, needed 199 yards to break O. J. Simpson's single-season rushing record of 2,003 yards, but fell far short with a pedestrian 47-yard day. It was all he could do just to get off the field after the sloppy game. "I wanted to get into the dressing room and get warm," he told a reporter for the *Chicago Sun-Times*.

The Giants weren't exactly sure-handed themselves, dropping two touchdown passes and a bushel of others from quarterback Joe Pisarcik.

"It was the sort of game both teams tried to give each other," Chicago safety Doug Plank said later.

And the teams went into the sudden-death period tied at 9–9.

The scoring in regulation, what little there was, went like this: Thomas kicked a 23-yard field goal for Chicago in the first quarter. Joe Danelo tied the game for New York with a 38-yard field goal later in the first quarter and put the Giants ahead 6–3 with a 19-yard kick in the fourth period. Robin Earl's four-yard touchdown run off left tackle with 6:02 remaining put the Bears on top 9–6 (Thomas's extra point try was blocked). The Giants tied the game and sent it into overtime on Danelo's 27-yarder with 38 seconds left.

"I remember trying a long field goal in overtime," says Thomas. "It was 40 or 45 yards in the ice, and the ball veered off to the left. I just started praying—no joking at all—I actually did, and said if it was Christ's will that we win the game, give me another chance to have things go right. We had been doing a good enough job ourselves in messing it up."

It took a while before Thomas's prayers were answered. The Bears tried another field goal, this one from 27 yards, but a bad snap from center resulted in a botched play.

It came down to the final seconds of overtime to decide this spill-a-minute contest. The Bears' winning drive started when they recovered their own fumble at the Giant 44-yard line. Avellini moved Chicago to the 25 with two smart passes. There, with 48 seconds left, he decided on a play called the "72 backs drag," whereby both Payton and backfield mate Roland Harper float out into the flat for a short pass. The ball went to Payton and he dragged it down to the 11, where he was stopped inside the sideline stripe. This was crucial, since the Bears had no more timeouts left and time was quickly running out when Payton was pulled down.

"After I caught the ball, I looked to the sideline and considered going out of bounds," Payton told *Chicago Tribune* writer Bob Logan. "But I saw an opportunity to break a tackle, and with 48 seconds left, I knew Thomas had time to kick the field goal."

Actually, there were less than 30 seconds left when Payton slithered to the 11 and was finally brought down to earth.

Then Pardee sent in Thomas and the field goal kicking team. And Thomas put the ball through the uprights from 28 yards out with eight seconds left.

"Those prayers I was saying on the sidelines must have worked," says Thomas. "My left foot stuck just as if it were a dry field and the ball went through the uprights. The left foot is the important one for a soccer-style kicker, you know, because that's your plant foot.

Even on the field goal I made earlier in the game, I made it in spite of my left foot slipping. On the winning kick, I watched the films later and just couldn't believe that the foot stuck the way it was supposed to."

Thomas was in a mental blizzard when he made the winning kick. There was just time enough to swing his right foot. Preparation was out of the question. As a matter of fact, so was thinking.

"On the earlier kicks we had more time, of course," Thomas remembers. "As a matter of fact on a couple of them, as I was trotting out on the field, Walter Payton and Roland Harper were down on their hands and knees trying to clear off some of that sleet and ice and snow that was in my path. On the winning one, we just ran out there and kicked it."

What followed could only be described as madness, the Polar Bear Club gone berserk on a wintry December day.

"There was just pandemonium on the field," remembers Thomas. "We were all rolling around in the slush for the next 15 minutes like little boys in mud."

After the loud joy, there was quiet contemplation.

"We all went into the locker room and prayed, thanking God that we came out with the victory."

Thomas was then besieged by reporters from newspapers and television. It was a unique experience for a kicker, who rarely gets the headlines like the backfield people. Not even at Notre Dame when he kicked the winning points for the national championship over Alabama did he experience attention like this.

"Those dramatic kicks, like the one in the Giant game, don't happen that often," Thomas says. "I had plenty of good kicking games at Notre Dame—once I kicked three field goals against Southern Cal, and that was a thrill. But never did I go into a game where it was in question upon my particular field goal until my last collegiate game. And then, playing against the no. 1

team [Alabama] for the national championship, it happened. And that was exciting!

"But the Giant game was special because of the adversity we had to go through to win it. There's something a little extra about having adversity staring you in the face and being able to come through and be successful in something like that. You know, it just gives you an extra charge."

ELROY "CRAZYLEGS" HIRSCH

These days the nickname "Crazylegs" might evoke myriad images—possibly anything from Farrah Fawcett's gams to the latest advertisement for a new pair of panty hose.

Back in the 1950s, it wasn't lasses, but strictly a guy who caught passes.

Crazylegs?

"Well, yes," says Elroy Hirsch. "My left foot points out farther than my right. So when I take a step with the left foot, it comes behind me and I have to swing it around to get it in front of me. I wobble, kinda. . . ."

Frances Powers, who used to write for the *Chicago Daily News*, gave Hirsch the crazy nickname after watching him run down the sidelines for Wisconsin against the Great Lakes service team in 1942.

"One of my feet was going one way, the other one in another direction on that run," Hirsch recalls. "I must have been a sight running down the sidelines."

Now athletic director at the University of Wisconsin, Hirsch still doesn't mind being called "Crazylegs." ("Any name is better than Elroy," he points out.) He has also been called one of the great players in National Football League history, a receiver of such exceptional skill that he is not only a member of the Hall of Fame but also on the all-time NFL All-Star team. Hirsch's greatest successes were with the Los Angeles Rams in the 1950s, when he was generally recognized as the premier end in pro football.

It was one day as a collegian, however, that he holds most dear in his bank of memories.

"The game that had the biggest effect on me was the College All-Star game in Chicago in 1946 against the Los Angeles Rams," Hirsch says. "Of course, I was scared to death, anyway. But when they introduce you in the starting lineup, you come out at one end of Soldier Field and trot through the goal posts and there are two big spotlights on you . . . and they had a crowd of about 100,000 there [actually, 97,380].

"And then you run up field and they play your school song. And they had a huge American flag drawn across one end of Soldier Field. That really got to me; you know, the school song, 'On, Wisconsin,' and the flag and the spotlight and the excitement of it all."

The best was yet to come for Hirsch. Not far into the game, he ran 68 yards for a touchdown. Later, he turned a 32-yard pass from Northwestern's Otto Graham into a 62-yard TD in the third quarter. And the College All-Stars upset the powerhouse Rams 16–0 as Hirsch ran away with the Most Valuable Player prize.

"My wife and parents were there," Hirsch recalls, "so that was a hell of a night for me. On top of everything else, I had been a first-round draft choice of the Rams. But I chose to go to the Chicago Rockets [of the old All-America Conference] because I got a better offer. It was kind of nice to rub it in. . . ."

Hirsch's performance wasn't entirely error-free.

"The first time I carried the ball was on an end run, and I fumbled it. But I recovered the fumble . . . it was a six- or eight-yard loss. And then later in the game, I had that big run from scrimmage for the touchdown, which I think is still the longest run from scrimmage in the All-Star game."

Hirsch dwells on that point, savoring it for the moment.

"That can't be broken, you know," he reminds you, "because there are no more All-Star games."

Despite Hirsch's spectacular run in the first quarter and a tough defense that held the defending world champions scoreless, the collegians were hardly the picture of confidence in the dressing room at halftime.

"We were winning 7–0 at the half and we all sat there and couldn't believe it," Hirsch recalls. "You know, here's the world champion Rams. They've got Bob Waterfield and Jim Benton, a great, great receiver, and Kenny Washington. God, they just had a hell of a football team, and here we were ahead of them. We kind of said, when is the roof going to fall in? It was that kind of feeling. I don't think we had a heck of a lot of confidence."

There was no feeling, either, that the pros weren't giving their best.

"Heck, no; I think they were going all the way," says Hirsch. "The Rams had Tom Harmon, and I remember he received a dislocated elbow, our guys were hitting so hard. And that surprised me that our guys were good enough to play with the pros. Of course it was an unusual All-Star team in that we had the servicemen coming back. They were more mature than the normal college team."

As far as college teams go, this one had to be one of the best ever. Many of the players were not only college stars, but also had played on strong service teams during World War II and were made eligible for the game, even though they were out of school. Some players, in fact, were back for a second or third appearance in the game. Hirsch, for one, had seen service with the El Toro Marines, a powerful aggregation not unlike a pro team.

Hirsch, himself, was a triple-threat halfback who

played on Harry Stuhldreher's fine Wisconsin team of 1942 and later for Michigan, where he signed up as a Marine trainee. As a member of the Wolverine athletic program, he won a letter not only in football, but basketball, baseball, and track as well—the only athlete in Michigan history to accomplish that feat.

But there would be even better days for Hirsch, especially after he struggled through three desultory years with the hapless Rockets, when he was immobilized for the most part with injuries. Why did he select the Rockets over the more established Rams? Purely economics, he says.

"I was getting married and I needed the money," he says. "The Rockets offered me a thousand dollars more than the Rams did. The Rams offered me a $5,000 contract with a $1,000 bonus, and I signed with the Rockets for $6,000 and a $1,000 bonus. Now that I think of it, I saved more that first year than I do now."

Money would not be the prime motivating factor when Hirsch later made movies ("Unchained," "Battle Cry," and "Crazylegs") and touchdowns in Los Angeles. When Hirsch's three-year contract ran out with the Rockets, he ran to the Rams in 1949, where he was greeted with open arms by Clark Shaughnessy. There, the Ram coach made a move that Hirsch insists "saved my life." Shaughnessy, aware of Hirsch's injury-weakened knee, put him on a daily running routine. Also aware of his penchant for fractured skulls (one of many injuries he had suffered with the Rockets), Shaughnessy contrived a special headgear for Hirsch to wear. Then Shaughnessy really did the most important thing he could do for Hirsch—he switched him from a halfback to an end. This not only added years to his career, but miles of yardage to his statistics.

Working with two of the game's greatest quarterbacks —Bob Waterfield and Norm Van Brocklin—Hirsch put new meaning into the passing game with his long-distance catches. The "bomb" became an explosive word in the pro football vocabulary, with Hirsch's familiar long-legged figure many a time outrunning a deep defender and settling under a touchdown pass, his back to the ball. In 1951 Hirsch established an NFL record of 1,495 yards on receptions. Amazingly, he did it in only 12 games. That same year he scored 17 touchdowns to tie the league record set by the great Don Hutson. In one period combining the 1950–51 seasons, Hirsch caught at least one touchdown pass through 11 games.

"We had an aerial circus at Los Angeles all right," says Hirsch, who might be considered the prototype of the modern-day flanker. "Waterfield was the best football player I have ever seen, all around. He was a great field general, did all of our passing, did all of our punting, he kicked off for us, he kicked field goals, he was one of the first guys to run the boot-leg. And then in my first game with the Rams, I was at safety and Bob Waterfield was a defensive right half. And in 1945, I didn't see Bob do this, but they said they put him on Hutson man for man. Of course Don was in his later years, but still Bob was on him."

Interestingly, it was Hirsch himself who made versatile players like Waterfield an extinct breed in the NFL. Hirsch's singularly unique talent of catching passes served to change the game to one of offensive and defensive specialization. Hirsch retired as an active player in 1957, and the NFL Hall of Fame gladly opened its doors for him in 1974.

"That was the biggest day for me, emotionally," says Hirsch. "That topped it all. Everybody breaks down and cries there. I know I did."

GALE SAYERS

Pride. It's a little word with a lot of meaning. "A sense of personal dignity," is the way one dictionary describes it, but each individual has his own definition.

Gale Sayers, for instance, will tell you: "When I was coming out of grade school, high school, and college, I thought to myself that I could be better than the Jimmy Browns and Paul Hornungs. And I went that route, imagining myself a better player. I didn't pattern myself after anyone. It was just a matter of going out there and getting myself in the best shape and just letting things go."

This attitude was obvious in a shining, if shortlived, career with the Chicago Bears. It sparked towering performances in Sayers, including a magnificent six-touchdown day against the San Francisco 49ers. It wasn't the game he remembers most, though. Two others stand out in his mind more, a 45–37 victory over the Minnesota Vikings in 1965 and a 24–16 triumph over the New York Giants in 1970.

And in both of those games, "pride" was the key word for this meteoric football star. Against Minnesota, Sayers had a strong personal reason to do well—he had been disparaged by Viking coach Norm Van Brocklin. Recalls Sayers.

"We had another young runner on our team, Andy Livingstone, a fullback out of Virginia College, a real, fine athlete, and it came out in the papers that Van Brocklin felt that Andy Livingstone could be a much greater athlete than Gale Sayers. So you never know how that works on your psyche, but probably in the back of my mind, it made me want to do well against the Vikings on that particular day."

Sayers did more than well: he scored four touchdowns, rushed for 64 yards, caught four passes for 63 more, completed a pass for 27 yards, and returned kickoffs for another 170 yards, including a 96-yard touchdown return to give the Bears the lead for good at 38–37 with 2:18 remaining in the game.

"That game meant more to me than the six-touchdown day against the 49ers," points out Sayers, "because every time I scored against San Francisco, we were ahead by two touchdowns or 17 points. So they really didn't need my scoring. We beat the 49ers 61–20. But the game against the Vikings sticks out more in my mind because it was more of a pressure situation. Going into the last two minutes, we were behind, and I ran the kickoff back and we were ahead. It went back and forth all the time. Every time they scored, I scored."

The game was played in partially cloudy, warm weather in Minneapolis on October 17, 1965. Sayers was not involved in any of the scoring in the first half, when Chicago held a 17–13 lead, but did all of it for the Bears after intermission.

A field goal by Fred Cox after 3:37 had elapsed in the third period cut Chicago's lead to 17–16, and Minnesota then went in front 23–17 less than eight minutes later on a 40-yard touchdown run by Bill Brown. With 20 seconds left in the third period, Sayers scored his first points of the day on an 18-yard TD pass from Rudy

Bukich. Now Chicago was in the lead again, at 24–23.

At the start of the fourth quarter, the Vikings took the lead once more, at 30–24, as quarterback Fran Tarkenton rolled out two yards for a touchdown to cap a 55-yard, eight-play drive. Now it was Chicago's turn, and the Bears moved ahead 31–20 on a 25-yard touchdown pass from Bukich to Sayers with nine minutes remaining.

This ping-pong action continued at a furious pace as the game headed toward its dramatic conclusion. With two minutes and 30 seconds left, Brown scored on a four-yard run to give the Vikings the lead again, 37–31. That margin only lasted about 12 seconds, or just about the time it took Sayers to gather up the kickoff at his four-yard line and run 96 yards for the Bears' go-ahead touchdown and a 38–37 lead. Roger Leclerc's extra-point kick actually provided the Bears with their winning point. On that game-winning kickoff return, Sayers followed a wedge of four blockers up the left sideline, outrunning a host of Viking defenders. The Vikings, actually, were prepared for the route that Sayers took—Van Brocklin even shouted orders for his players to plug the lane—but were enable to stop him.

But Sayers wasn't finished yet. With 1:32 remaining, Dick Butkus intercepted a Tarkenton pass and returned it 35 yards to the Minnesota ten-yard line. Sayers then went over right guard with 52 seconds on the clock to complete the Bears' victory in one of the most exciting games ever played in the National Football League.

For personal glory, Sayers's game against the Giants on September 19, 1970, could not match the one against Minnesota. But for personal satisfaction, it did.

"Some people will look at the statistics and say that I didn't have a good day," says Sayers, who totaled only 43 yards rushing on 17 attempts. "But I was called on to run the ball in several third-and-one, third-and-two situations, and I picked up the yards we needed on these third-down situations. The yards kept a drive going or ran down the clock, so I got a great deal of satisfaction from that. Although I didn't have the big yardage day, we still won the game. Also, I was hurting a little bit at the time."

Sayers personally accounted for five first downs that day, two of them keeping alive scoring drives. On a third-and-two situation with less than 30 seconds to play in the half, the Chicago halfback ran for a first down that eventually led to a Matt Percival field goal that cut the Giants' lead at intermission to 13–10. On a third-and-three late in the third period, Sayers once again picked up a first down to lead to Jack Concannon's quarterback sneak that gave the Bears a 17–13 lead and their eventual winning point.

That Sayers was running at all in 1970 was extraordinary. Few had counted on his coming back from a savage knee injury in 1968, when he was put out of action by San Francisco cornerback Kermit Alexander.

"Everyone counted me out after that game," Sayers says. "They felt that no one could come back from a knee injury at full strength. But I put some added pressure on myself, saying I know I can do this if I work hard enough during the off-season. I had faith in the doctor who performed the surgery [Dr. Theodore Fox], and I knew I could do it. I knew I could come back."

Sayers not only came back, he came back strong. He wound up leading the league in rushing, the only man to go over 1,000 yards in 1969 with 1,032. He also returned kickoffs for 339 yards and caught passes for 116 more.

"I got off to a slow start," Sayers remembers, "and I got some bad press early. They were saying that I wasn't as fast, that I wasn't cutting like I did in 1968. But I was determined to show them. The thing that made that season so outstanding for me was that we had a 1–13 record. We won just one ballgame all year, and that put added pressure on me. Not winning and trying to do well individually was a big burden."

This kind of success was even sweeter considering Sayers's inauspicious transition to the pros from his great college days at Kansas. He was always fighting to prove himself, it seemed. Even before he joined the Bears, he had a less-than-glittering reputation as the result of a misunderstanding with Otto Graham, the coach of the College All-Star team in 1965. This was at the time of the All-Stars' annual game with the pros in Chicago.

"I got hurt in practice," says Sayers. "I either sprained my knee or twisted it, I don't remember exactly what happened. Anyway, they took x-rays, and they couldn't find anything wrong with it. But the thing hurt; I couldn't cut. And so I think Graham got the idea that I was loafing and didn't want to play in the game. By game time, I was healthy 100 percent and wanted to play, but he chose not to play me."

Graham later voiced the opinion that Sayers wouldn't make it in pro football. But Sayers, his pride showing, was of the opinion that he would. And so was Chicago Bears owner George Halas.

"I went in to see George Halas," Sayers says, "and I told him what happened, the circumstances leading up to my not playing in the All-Star game. And George Halas said, 'Gale, that's behind you. All we're concerned with is what you do from this day on.' When I knew that the incident would not affect my relationship with the head coach–owner of the team, I put that all behind me. I thought from that day on, I would try to be the best football player I could."

The determination was wholly evident in Sayers's first year with the Bears, when he produced 22 touchdowns and led the NFL in scoring with 132 points, both records for a rookie. In addition, he rushed for 867 yards, caught 29 passes for 507, and returned kickoffs for 660 yards more. In 1967 he led the league in rushing with 1,231 yards and in kickoff returns with 718 and caught 34 passes for 447 yards in a breathtaking triple-threat performance.

Sayers continued to make high marks in these categories, even in 1968, although he missed the last five games because of his celebrated injury. Despite playing only nine games that season, he was still a unanimous NFL selection by his peers, an acknowledgment of his greatness.

In 1969 Sayers's expensive knee held up under the pounding of 14 NFL games, and his performance marked the first time on record that any running back had made the 1,000-plus yards total the season immediately following knee surgery. The Pro Football Writers gave Sayers the George Halas Award for being the most courageous player, but Sayers in turn gave the award to his roommate and close friend, Brian Piccolo, who was to die of cancer on June 16, 1970. Their sensitive relationship inspired the popular movie, "Brian's Song."

Sayers suffered a preseason injury to his left knee in 1970, and it proved to be a fatal one for his football career. He only played two games that season, including the aforementioned game against the Giants. He retired after another lame season in 1971 and went home to Kansas where he became assistant athletic director at his alma mater. Later he moved up to the athletic director's chair at Southern Illinois University, a position he holds today, bringing to it the same kind of fervor he had in the pros. Sixteen-hour days and six-day weeks are not uncommon for him at Carbondale—the same type of regimen he followed in the pros when he was anything but a prima donna.

Talking about his compulsion to excel in all phases of the game, not just running, Sayers says: "I was getting paid to play football. I thought that was part of my job, to run back punts and kickoff returns."

It wasn't so much that Sayers had a suicidal bent, as some do on pro football's specialty teams today, but a passion to help in all areas that he could.

"I ran back kickoff returns and punt returns in college, and I enjoyed running those back mainly because when I was with the Bears, that was part of our offense. That was an offensive play, just like at the line of scrimmage. And I enjoyed it because you could score in a matter of seconds. You can give your team good field position when you're running back a kickoff or a punt because everyone is in front of you, so if you have good peripheral vision you can see what's going on. It was part of my downfall, because I got hurt on a kickoff return one time. But I enjoyed it, I really did."

Sayers also had a penchant for running inside, a seemingly unusual leaning for a scatback. But there was a method to his madness.

"I enjoyed going through the line," he says, "mainly because it was a more direct route. Once you break the first line of tacklers, the front four, the linebackers, you only have one or two men to contend with. I always felt that I could beat one man 100 percent of the time and beat two men 80 percent of the time. If I burst into the secondary, I'm going to get me 30, 40 yards, if not a touchdown. Coming around end, you have everybody coming at you. That's how I got my first knee injury. Everybody is flowing your way. And if you try to cut back, you're coming back to the flow of the tacklers. So it's much tougher going around end. You exert all that energy going around end to gain two or three yards. I'd rather exert that energy going up the middle to gain two with the possibility of breaking for 80."

As it was, Sayers exerted enough energy just running the way he did with his hectic, crazy-quilt style.

"I think if you drew a straight line down the middle of the field, most running backs wouldn't deviate from the line probably more than one or two degrees," says

Sayers in explaining his running style. "I might deviate 25, 30, 40 degrees from either side of that line. I used more leg and head and shoulder fakes. Most backs today use burning speed. I didn't have burning speed. I had some speed. But my biggest asset was my quickness. See the hole, get in the hole, make a move, and get out. I tried to use as much of the football field as I could to my advantage."

And he did it boldly, generally unaware of reputations and surroundings.

"I remember in my rookie year when we played the Giants in New York, we were riding to Yankee Stadium and a writer for the *Tribune* asked me how did it feel playing in New York," Sayers says. "But I wasn't thinking too much about that. A football field's 50 yards wide and 100 yards long, and I didn't really care where we played. Some people are concerned about playing in various cities. Hey, you know, when I was on that football field, I was thinking about one thing: my plays, my assignment, can we win. I wasn't concerned with anything else."

Only once in his career did Sayers feel awed by the setting.

"The only time I was really caught up in a game that way," he says, "was in my rookie year when we played the Baltimore Colts and I was sitting on the sidelines watching Johnny Unitas bring the Colts down the field in the last couple of seconds. That was the only time I was really awed, because I remember sitting in my living room in high school seeing Johnny Unitas, Raymond Berry, and Lenny Moore on television, and now I'm playing against these people. And I was sitting there, with the defense in there, thinking, 'Hey, I've finally made it. I'm finally playing against these people.' "

It didn't take Sayers long to get rid of that hero-worshipping attitude, though.

"Once you get knocked on your butt, you forget

about it," says Sayers. "I don't care how great the other guy is. He's trying to beat you, so you better go out and do your job."

LYLE ALZADO

The picture comes into sharp focus now in Lyle Alzado's memory: coach Red Miller standing in the middle of a crush of orange jerseys delivering a Hall of Fame pep talk.

"I love you," Miller is telling the Denver Broncos. "Play for yourselves because I love you and play for the fans in Colorado. This is your chance. This is the moment we've worked for all these years. You've waited 16 years for this opportunity and here it is right before you."

"It was just unbelievable," says Alzado. "He had me crying . . . he had guys crying. He just had us ready to go through a wall."

That memorable moment happened just before the Broncos took the field against the Oakland Raiders for the National Football League's American Conference championship game in the 1977 season. Significantly, it was the highest plateau that the Broncos had ever reached in their history. That fact was not lost on Alzado, whose entire career was part of the Broncos' bitter past.

So this game was really special.

"I had been there seven years," points out one of the

NFL's best defensive ends, now with the Cleveland Browns. "We had been through seasons where we won three, four, five games. It was very frustrating. Even in 1977 no one expected us to win or go as far as we did in the playoffs . . . and here we are playing for the AFC championship."

And winning it, 20–17.

"That was definitely the most exciting moment I've had as an athlete," emphasizes the 6-foot-3, 250-pounder from Brooklyn, N. Y. "You know, Oakland had been the Super Bowl champions the year before and they had been dominant in the division—I don't know how many years—10 out of 13 or so. So no one expected us to win."

That included the television people, Alzado remembers with amusement.

"When we reached the locker room after the game, it was kind of funny because the TV people had all their equipment in Oakland's locker room because they thought the Raiders would win. They didn't have any cameras set up in our locker room. They had to come in with the portable stuff to do their interviews. Then they did a few and left."

The game had all the sound and fury usually associated with one of such magnitude. The players had the fury, the Denver fans the sound.

"It was like being in a street fight," Alzado remembers. "The fans were just screaming and yelling . . . you couldn't hear yourself think."

Luckily for the Broncos, the game was played in Denver before the vociferous, adoring fans who had taken the so-called "Orange Crush" to their hearts that year.

"They were very instrumental in our success," Alzado points out. "Every time we took the field for a home game, the noise was just unbelievable. And even when we went to away games, they came to the airport. There'd be thousands of them waiting for us, cheering us on. It was incredible."

The fervor of these fans was expressed in a variety of ways—one family went so far as to disfigure the family car to display their affection for the Broncos.

"Before the AFC title game with Oakland, this family came over to the practice field in an orange-colored station wagon. Are you ready for this? They had all the guys on the team sign their names on the car!"

The team was honored with a pregame parade through downtown Denver, a ceremony usually associated with postgame festivities. But the citizens of Denver had good reason for being enthusiastic about their team's new status in the NFL. A contending role had always been foreign to the Bronco franchise.

"I wish I could give you the feeling that everyone had that year in Denver," Alzado says, "because it was awesome . . . just awesome. It was really something, the way everybody on our team felt about each other that year. We knew what we were finally accomplishing after 16 years of nothing."

Alzado had been associated with many fine players in his previous years with the Broncos, including the effervescent Floyd Little, a bow-legged scatback who ranked with the best in NFL history. But all Little and Alzado had to show for several years of hard work was dirty uniforms.

Long overdue personal recognition finally came to Alzado along with team success in 1977, when the brilliant defensive end was selected as a starter in the Pro Bowl and given some prestigious individual awards. The Broncos' high-profile season naturally encouraged this recognition, but actually Alzado had been excelling ever since he was drafted out of Yankton (S.D.) College in 1971. Herculean strength (he has deadlifted 595 pounds) and quickness afoot have made him one of the NFL's premier pass rushers in the past decade. In 1978, when Alzado was selected first team All-Pro for the second straight year, he recorded a club-leading nine quarterback sacks. Alzado's ferocity on the field belies his true nature, which has earned him a raft of humanitarian awards for his civic work.

Except for 1976, a lost year because of a knee injury on the season's first play, Alzado was a starter in Denver since the first game of his rookie season. He played in more than 100 games, including the playoffs, and most of the contests blur together. Except for the 1977 game with Oakland, of course.

"It's funny," Alzado recalls, "but during that week, no athlete from either team that I remember had made a derogatory statement about the other team, for fear that it would end up on somebody's bulletin board. Sometimes it does. When you say something bad about a team or an individual, it ends up in that locker room and guys look at it and say, 'Okay, let's kick his. . . .' But nobody said anything bad from either team, so you knew it was going to be a hell of a battle."

And it was.

"I played against probably the best tackle in football that year in Art Shell," says Alzado. "It was just a very physical, brutal game—probably the toughest game physically that I've ever been in. It was a very tough battle for me against Shell especially, and I'd call it a draw. He'd beat me, I'd beat him. He'd beat me, I'd beat him . . . it was that simple. It was a brutal matchup for me."

The Oakland running game wasn't any easier for Alzado to handle.

"It was awesome. No matter who you are or what you are, it was very difficult to stop. Behind Art Shell and their other guys, their running game was as good as any in the NFL at that time."

Using a grind-it-out style, the Raiders had a habit of keeping the ball for long periods of time. On their first two possessions in the championship game, they seemed to have the ball forever—using up more than eight minutes during a total of 18 plays. Shell and guard Gene

Upshaw were two of the main elements in Oakland's offensive thrust, clearing huge holes for Pete Banazak to dart through. Still, when it counted, the bearded, animated Alzado and his defensive teammates held the Oakland charge. When the Raiders moved down to the Denver three-yard line in the first quarter, the Broncos allowed them no further penetration. Oakland had to settle for Earl Mann's 20-yard field goal.

The second time they had the ball, the Raiders pushed slowly and inexorably down to the Bronco 12. Stopped there by the fired-up Denver defense, the Raiders were again forced to try a field goal, but this time failed.

All the while, during both of the Raiders' early drives, Alzado was obviously enflamed.

"At times, Alzado appeared to be lecturing the Raiders, pointing, gesturing and babbling away, particularly at tackle Art Shell," observed a *Sports Illustrated* writer.

This type of leadership also enflamed the Denver defense, which held the Raiders to merely three points in the game's first 18½ minutes—even though Oakland had possession of the ball for more than 16 minutes of that time.

Meanwhile, the Denver offense was working more efficiently, taking less time to score more points as quarterback Craig Morton zipped a pass to Haven Moses that turned into a 74-yard touchdown play. So Denver took a 7–3 lead into the dressing room at halftime, while most of the 74,982 fans at Mile High Stadium roared their approval.

While the fans raged on the field, the Broncos were a quiet counterpoint in their dressing room, Alzado recalls.

"It was really different for a change, because the entire locker room was just silent. Normally, you go in, everyone's talking, trying to go over everything together. But nobody said anything this time. The coaches went over a few things with us, and everybody just looked at each other and kind of nodded. There wasn't a word spoken in that locker room. It was just like we knew what was before us and what we had to accomplish. That was it . . . we just went right back on the field and did it."

Before they "did it," though, they did make some defensive changes.

"We made some adjustments to stop their running game a little more and put some more pressure on Kenny Stabler [the Oakland quarterback]," Alzado recalls.

In the third period that wonderful defense set up Denver's second touchdown of the day when Brison Manor recovered a fumble on the Oakland 17. Not long thereafter, Jon Keyworth took a pitchout from Morton on the two and raced into the end zone for a 14–3 Bronco lead.

Denver's muscular defense was later instrumental in setting up another touchdown—and this one, in the fourth quarter, turned out to be the game winner. After Oakland had cut Denver's lead to 14–10 on a Stabler touchdown pass early in the final quarter, a blitz by Alzado and company forced the Raider quarterback to throw an interception. The ball landed in the hands of Bronco linebacker Bob Swenson, giving Denver possession on the Oakland 17, and a little while later Morton hit Moses with another touchdown pass. That gave the Broncos a 20–10 lead and enough of a cushion to withstand another TD pass by Stabler.

The new AFC champions then rushed off the field to their dressing room to "pray and celebrate."

"Denver was a very religious team," Alzado says. "Before the game we'd pray, and after the game we'd pray. Before we did any celebrating, that's what we did. And then all hell broke loose. Everybody was kicking each other and clapping, and there was lots of champagne being spilled."

And lots of dreams coming true.
"I wish I could draw you a picture," says Alzado.
Like they say, you had to be there.

JOHNNY UNITAS

Johnny Unitas, once the quarterback of quarterbacks, can reach back and toss around memories as well as anyone.

"I can still see Lenny Moore making that great cut and George Preas leading him in for the touchdown," says Unitas. "That was some run."

It was some game, too, the one between the Baltimore Colts and San Francisco 49ers in 1958. If you were a Colt fan, of course. Baltimore was losing 27–7 at the half but came back to win 35–27 and wrap up the National Football League's Western Division title.

It is clearly Unitas's favorite game, no matter what they say about the subsequent victory over the New York Giants for the world championship, the contest some have called "the greatest game ever played." Unitas is united in his thinking with Lenny Moore, who also makes the San Francisco game of '58 his no. 1 pick in another part of this book (see page 15).

"Yeah, the '58 game with the Giants was a fine football game," says Unitas, now owner of the Golden Arm restaurant in Baltimore. "But the best thing . . . was the last two minutes when we drove down to tie the game, and then of course the overtime. It was the first overtime

113

ever. Up until then, it was a good football game, but as far as I'm concerned, not as great as a lot of people thought."

What made the 49er game more special in Unitas's estimation were the tremendous odds the Colts had to overcome to win.

"Our defense had to play a fantastic game in the second half," says Unitas, "and we had to score four touchdowns while we shut them out. That wasn't easy—shutting them out, I mean. But our defense held people like Hugh McElhenny and Y. A. Tittle and Joe Perry scoreless, and we were fortunate enough to score 28 points."

Unitas remembers seeing two different Baltimore teams that day: a bad one in the first half, and a great one in the second.

"Even though we were losing by 20 points at the half, we never thought we were out of it," Unitas says. "I just knew that I played badly in the first half. I threw one pass right before the half ended and Matt Hazletine intercepted, and they scored a touchdown to put them up 27–7. Leo Nomellini came through our line like a fire truck and deflected my pass right into Hazletine's arms around our six-yard line, and Matt just walked in for the score. Meanwhile, I was laying flat on my back, smothered by Nomellini. It wasn't very enjoyable. We did get some hope, though, when Ordell Braase blocked their extra-point attempt. And the second half was another game entirely. We kind of controlled the football, scored some good touchdowns, and then finally went on to win it in the last minute or two."

The game ranked as the most glorious comeback in the history of the franchise, since the Colts had never in history been down by 20 points at the half and come back to win. They didn't need any encouragement in the dressing room at halftime, either, from coach Weeb Ewbank. All were aware of the significance of the contest.

"Weeb didn't say a whole lot," Unitas recalls. "He just put the score on the blackboard and said we needed 21 points to win. That was it. If the defense would shut them out, and we scored 21 points, we would win."

And if the Pittsburgh Steelers would beat the Chicago Bears that afternoon, then a Baltimore victory would mean the divisional championship. Which is exactly what happened.

As the Colts started their comeback in the third period, they heard the news over the loudspeaker that the Steelers had indeed beaten the Bears. The Colts had just scored a touchdown on a 62-yard, 13-play drive capped by Alan Ameche's one-yard plunge to cut San Francisco's lead to 27–14.

"Ameche, our big fullback, really helped us get going," Unitas recalls. "I remember we had a fourth and one on the 41-yard line of the 49ers, and Ameche got us the yardage for the first down. Not long after that, Ameche scored and that really gave us a big lift."

The Colts got another big lift from their defense, which got the ball back for them in a hurry on a pass interception by safety Ray Brown in the end zone. And Unitas didn't waste any time cashing in on the situation.

Unitas and Jim Mutscheller hooked up on a 50-yard pass play on which the receiver "made a great catch," according to the Baltimore quarterback. "That was some play by Mutscheller," says Unitas. "Then I passed to Raymond Berry for 16 more to move the ball close to their goal line, and the Horse [Ameche] took it in again." Ameche scored from one yard out, and now only six points (27–21) separated the Colts from the 49ers. Braase's block of the San Francisco PAT in the first half began to look bigger every minute.

"There was still plenty of time left, something like 11 minutes," Unitas remembers.

For this all-world quarterback, that indeed was enough time to pull out a game. Last-minute victories were Unitas's specialties, anyway.

The crowd of 57,557 at Baltimore's Memorial Stadium stirred uneasily for a while, but the murmurs soon became roars when Moore took off on his game-winning 73-yard touchdown run just a few minutes from the end.

"It wasn't anything fancy," Unitas says, "I just lined him up at halfback and called a sweep to the left. When I gave the handoff to Lenny, our left guard and tackle, Art Spinney and Jim Parker, really did a heck of a job knocking down the San Francisco line. And Moore got a terrific block from Ameche as he turned the corner. Then Lenny got another block from Berry. It was a beaut."

Moore put on a twisting move to shake free of the cornerback, then headed for the middle of the field and followed Preas into the end zone.

"That was it—73 yards and a touchdown. That tied the game at 27–27 and nobody probably remembers, but Steve Myhra kicked the extra point which turned into the winning point."

The score was now 28–27 in favor of the Colts, but Unitas wasn't finished yet. The defense, acting up again, got the ball back once more for him with an intercepted pass by Carl Taseff. And 11 plays later, Unitas had the Colts in the 49er end zone with a honey of a pass to Berry.

About that game-wrapping play, Unitas recalls he first had some trouble figuring it out.

"I didn't know what to do," remembers Unitas, "so I went over to the sidelines to speak to Weeb about it. Well, he wouldn't say anything to me, and I kept following him down the sidelines, and he never really gave me anything definite. The whole thing was really funny. He was walking away from me and I was trying to catch him to find out what he wanted me to do; and he would turn and walk the other way, and I would turn around and follow him and keep asking him what did he want to do. And he never said anything. So I got upset at the time and said, 'Hell, I'll get something myself.' "

The situation was a third and long on the Colts' 40-yard line, and what Unitas finally decided to do was throw a pass. It went for a touchdown.

"Really, the defense won the game for us," Unitas stresses. "We should have cut the ball up into little slices and given it to each of our defensive players. Let's face it—they turned the game around. This happened when the 49ers had a fourth-and-one situation on their 40-yard line in the last quarter. Tittle gave the ball to McElhenny, and our defense stopped him cold. They were forced to punt, and not long after that, Lenny made that fantastic run."

Late heroics were a hallmark of Unitas's career, of course. Few quarterbacks in history could do as much with as little time as Unitas could. Witness his classic performance in the championship game against the Giants in 1958, when he deftly moved the Colts from their own 14-yard line into range for Myhra's tying field goal with less than two minutes left.

Unitas opened his quarterbacking career in Baltimore in 1956 by throwing an interception for a touchdown to J. C. Caroline of the Chicago Bears on October 21, 1956. He closed it in Baltimore with a touchdown pass to Eddie Hinton on December 3, 1972. In between, he filled the air with footballs and the books with records that may never be surpassed.

Unitas ended his 18-year career in San Diego in 1973, ranked number one in NFL history in five career categories: most touchdown passes (290); most yards gained passing (40,239); most seasons with 3,000 yards or more passing (3); most passes attempted (5,186); and most passes completed (2,830). He established 22 records during his stay in Baltimore and was named the NFL's Most Valuable Player three times. Perhaps his most re-

markable individual achievement is his mark of most
consecutive games with a touchdown pass—47—a
record that ranks with the most sacred in American
sports history. Unitas was named the Player of the Decade in the 1960s in one prestigious poll, and during 1969
he won the balloting as the greatest player in the first 50
years of pro football.

Ironically, had it not been for some faith on the part
of the Baltimore organization, this glittering career never would have gotten off the ground.

Born in Pittsburgh in 1933, the second of four children, Unitas's early life was hardly luxurious. His
father, driver of a coal delivery truck, died when John
was relatively young, and his mother was forced to raise
the family. He excelled on a local high school football
team, St. Justin's, and hoped for a scholarship to Notre
Dame. But he was rejected there because of his size (5-
foot-11, 140 pounds) and instead settled for the University of Louisville. Although Unitas did well there, pro
teams were not especially enamored of him, and the
Pittsburgh Steelers waited until the ninth round of the
1955 draft to select him. Unitas, newly married, needed
the work at the time, but the Steelers cut him loose after
a brisk and shallow inspection.

To keep active in football, Unitas played in a semipro
league in Pittsburgh for $6 a game in what must rank as
one of the gloomiest periods of his life. This depressing
state, however, lasted only as long as it took Don Kellett
to make a phone call to Unitas's house in February of
1956. Kellett, the general manager of the Colts at the
time, invited Unitas to come to Baltimore for a tryout in
the spring. He did—and won the role of backup quarterback behind George Shaw. Later that season, Shaw was
injured in a game with the Chicago Bears, and Unitas
became the regular quarterback, a job he would hold
firmly in the palm of his talented right hand for many
years.

When Unitas first joined the Colts, they had never

had a winning season. But after his first year with them, they never had a losing one. Within two years he had the Colts winning the first of their two consecutive league championships.

And those great Baltimore teams of the late 1950s?

"Comparable to any that won titles," says Unitas. "I have no doubt of that—any team."

Unitas of course had something to do with that.

HAROLD CARMICHAEL

At Southern University, Harold Carmichael not only was a player's player, but a coach's dream. As Al Tabor so colorfully puts it: "If you were going to play football, you sure couldn't load the bus and not have Harold Carmichael on it."

Carmichael "came to play," as they say in the football vernacular. It was one particular day, though, that he came to play sick, and therein lies the story of his most memorable game.

The week before a contest with Arkansas AM&N, Southern's fine wide receiver was grounded with a flu ailment that hit Carmichael harder than any tackle that season.

"My temperature was up to 104 degrees," Carmichael remembers, "and I spent the whole week in the infirmary. I wasn't supposed to play that weekend, I was so sick."

But, as Tabor said, it was hard to keep Carmichael off the bus, especially when the team loaded to drive off to Pine Bluff, Arkansas. Carmichael went along, but not only for the ride.

"Sometimes you know just how far you can go,"

Carmichael says. "There's sick and there's *deathly* sick.
I wasn't deathly sick."

Carmichael packed enough antibiotics to open up his
own pharmacy.

"You could tell he was sick coming up," says Tabor,
then the Southern coach and later a scout for the Cleveland Browns. "Harold was very quiet, and he didn't say
much during the pregame meal, either."

Carmichael remembers: "By the time I got to the
game, I was feeling a little better, but I still had the high
temperature. And I couldn't eat; I was really weak by
game time."

Evidently not too weak, though, to catch a bunch of
passes, including one in the last minute that gave Southern a thrill-packed 17–10 victory.

The game was played in 1970, Carmichael's last year
in college, before he became a pass-catching whiz with
the Philadelphia Eagles.

Carmichael's catch of the winning touchdown pass
against Arkansas AM&N reflected a style that would
carry through his glorious NFL career. He went up like
a basketball player to get the pass, a characteristic ma-
neuver for the exceedingly tall (6-foot-8) Carmichael.

"It was a little turn-in pattern," Carmichael remembers, "and it was kind of a high-thrown ball and I had
to jump for it. I came down, and I hit one guy and just
went 40 yards for the score."

When Carmichael crossed the goal line to break a 10–
10 tie, there were only five seconds remaining. "It was
something I'll never forget," he says. "It was just a great
moment in my life that I was able to play in a situation
like that. The way I was feeling, to come off the bench
and help win the game was just one of my biggest
thrills."

For the record, the pass was thrown by quarterback
Jerome Bettis, a reserve whom Tabor had pulled off the
bench only moments before the winning score. On

Bettis's first play from scrimmage, he sent fullback Grover Richardson into the line, but Richardson ran around in circles and lost six yards. Bettis then hit Carmichael about 15 yards beyond the line of scrimmage, and the big end flashed through the Arkansas AM&N defenders.

"It was a quick slant pattern," Tabor recalls of the play. "We set it up on the sidelines. We had the one play left, and knew we had to go to Carmichael with it."

Although Carmichael remembers that he had been "playing off and on in the game, but not very much," he played long enough to catch an earlier touchdown pass for Southern.

"That was a standard quick out," Tabor remembers. "There was no problem there. Also, early in the ballgame, when we were controlling the ball, Harold caught about six passes to get us into scoring position. But we got down close and started using the ground game and fumbled."

Carmichael's winning touchdown catch capped a frantic finish to this exciting game, which had a lot of action packed into the last three minutes. In that span, the Southern defense stopped an Arkansas AM&N drive that threatened to break the 10–10 tie earlier. A field goal attempt was smothered when the Southern defense, including soon-to-be-pros Isiah Robertson and Jim Osborne, swarmed all over the Arkansas AM&N kicker.

Along with Carmichael and the aforementioned players, a lot of other NFL talent came out of that game. Playing for Arkansas AM&N that day were such as L. C. Greenwood, Wallace Francis, Terry Nelson, and Cleo Miller.

"At the time Harold was at Southern," says Tabor, "our league [the Southwestern Athletic Conference] was at its zenith for producing pro players. There are still good people coming out, but not like it was then "

Carmichael, of course, has been one of the biggest pro names to come out of that region. Born in Jacksonville, Florida, in 1949, Carmichael was a four-sport star at William M. Raines High School there before enrolling at Southern, a tradition-filled school with a handsome, sprawling campus hard by the Mississippi River in Baton Rouge, Louisiana.

Tabor immediately put his obvious talents to good use.

"He had been a high school quarterback," Tabor recalls. "He probably could throw the ball farther than anybody on our squad. But he had such rare hands that you wanted somebody throwing the ball to him, not him throwing to somebody who couldn't catch it as well."

Carmichael totaled 86 receptions as a collegian, including some of the most spectacular catches that Tabor had ever seen.

"To me, the greatest ball he ever caught was in a game against North Carolina A&T in Yankee Stadium," Tabor says. "That was early in 1970. The ball was really overthrown, way overthrown, and he just reached up and made the catch. It was fantastic. You knew that he was something rare, and it was a pleasure to have practice to see him perform. He developed this technique early of catching the ball and breaking a tackle. He could go up and get it."

Had it not been for some direction from Tabor, it's possible that Carmichael might have taken the wrong road on his professional career.

"He really wanted to play basketball pretty badly," Tabor remembers. "He was a good basketball player and he felt he could have made the National Basketball Association, and he probably could have. But I told him in the NBA at 6-foot-8 you're just an ordinary person; in football, you'd be the tallest receiver in the league. And so he acquiesced to that. He did play basketball in his senior year at Southern and helped the team tremendously. But his future was set for football."

And what a future that became after Carmichael was drafted by the Eagles on the seventh round in 1971. Carmichael became a starter in 1973 and caught a club-record and NFL-leading 67 passes that year. Since then he has averaged 52 catches and seven touchdowns every season since. In 1979 Carmichael established the all-time NFL record for most consecutive regular season games with receptions—112. He broke Danny Abramowicz's mark of 105 midway through the season and continued to build on the Herculean record as the Eagles moved into the playoffs for the second straight year.

"He's a tremendous physical talent," says Eagles' quarterback Ron Jaworski. "In the goal-line area, he's almost impossible to stop if you give him single coverage, even by someone as tall as 6-foot-3. That's why we spend a lot of time in our goal-line preparation every week. Harold and I work all the time on the Alley Oop pass over the shorter guy and the quick out or quick slant. Once we see the cornerback set up, we instinctively know exactly what we're going to do. We've developed real confidence in each other. He knows where I'm going to throw the ball, and I know what type of route he's going to run."

Carmichael's height is a distinct advantage in professional football, but not the only reason that he stands head and shoulders above most NFL receivers. In a recent interview with Bill Lyon of the *Philadelphia Inquirer*, Carmichael pointed out:

"People have been coming up to me for years and telling me I should catch everything thrown in my area. It looks like it should be simple. I know that. But anybody who thinks it's easy never played this game. I really believe that height makes no difference. Now I know people are going to think that's silly. Oh, sure, there are some plays where it helps. But there's so much more involved.

"Quarterbacks don't throw the ball high every time. For one thing, they don't always have the time. Plus, you've still got to get off the line, you've got to run your route right, the ball has to be thrown where you can catch it, and then you've still got great athletes to beat. It's not like it's just you and the passer. There are 21 other guys out there, and 11 of them are trying to stop you."

Along with his natural abilities, Carmichael has shown remarkable staying power in the pros, not having missed a game since 1972. It's just like college, really: he's wedded to football, in sickness or in health.

AHMAD RASHAD

With O. J. Simpson, the running play was the thing for the Buffalo Bills in 1974.

"We didn't throw the ball much," remembers Ahmad Rashad. "We had the best blocking in the league and also the best running back who ever played the game. Even third and twelve, we were running."

The pass might have been an endangered species on this team, but it wasn't yet extinct. Rashad's 36 receptions that year will attest to that.

One catch, in particular, will stay with him as long as he remembers his football career. It not only helped the Bills pull out a game against the Oakland Raiders but gave Rashad an extremely high profile.

"I run into people all over the country who come up to me and say they remember that game and that particular catch more so than any other thing I've done since," says Rashad, "and I guess that's why the game loomed so big to me. It's like that was my game to make me known to all football fans."

Observers not only remember The Catch, but also The Move that went along with it. Rashad describes it as a "tourjeté, kind of a reverse ballet move. It's a reverse spin kind of deal, you know, where you're running for-

ward and you take kind of a step out and you completely reverse yourself. It's almost a 360-degree turn. I went
down and out and spun back inside and the ball was
right back inside."

The Move was especially sweet, because not only did
it result in a touchdown play and a 21–20 victory over
the Raiders, but it came against perhaps the best cornerback in football at the time, Willie Brown.

"It was probably my best move ever on Willie," says
Rashad. "I had a touchdown earlier in the game against
the other cornerback; it was kind of a quick break-in
pattern. Against Brown, it was a quicker break-in, a
slant."

Adding to everything else was the glow of a national
spotlight. The contest was the weekly Monday night
game, the opener of the season in fact, and was seen by
countless millions of fans across the country.

"The Monday night game then was *the* game, you
know, *the* time to play," says Rashad. "Now it's gotten
a little bit different. I don't know if that comes with age
or not. But back then, I was really excited about it."

For sheer thrills, Rashad says, nothing since has quite
matched the excitement of that game with Oakland, nor
the season that unfolded after it.

"That particular season was the most exciting of my
career and that game was the height of it," says Rashad.
"Two years later, I went to the Super Bowl [with the
Minnesota Vikings] and caught a lot of passes. But in
1974, we had O. J. Simpson, and O. J. and I were room-
mates and it was like living with a legend. The team was
the best group of guys I've ever been around; I mean
really a closely-knit team. We were together all the time.
And the town was really behind us. You couldn't go
anywhere without getting mobbed by people. Even guys
who didn't even play much had a tough time going out
in public. The city of Buffalo was just really behind the
team, and Lou Saban was one of the greatest coaches
I've ever played for.

"You knew that everybody was going to be working hard. It was that kind of atmosphere. You had respect for everybody on the team. You knew it was going to be a joint effort every week. And when you win like that, in one of those group-type efforts, it's just a good feeling all around the locker room. I've had much better individual games than the one I had against Oakland that year, but not the whole group-effort feeling that I got from that one."

That "group-effort" feeling started for Rashad the minute he left his apartment for the game in Buffalo.

"I can remember driving to the stadium and everybody waving for 50 miles," says Rashad. "Everybody seemed to be going to the game that day, and they were all waving and wishing us luck. It was just total excitement . . . it was more exciting than the Super Bowl, way more exciting."

After suiting up, it got even more exciting for Rashad.

"When they introduced the offense and we took the field," he recalls, "I felt like my feet weren't even touching the ground. I don't think I've ever been as ready to play a football game as I was that night. I don't think I've ever been on that level too many times."

That game, and that season, set the tone for Rashad's career. Although he was injured and unable to play in 1975, Rashad eventually developed into one of the National Football League's most feared wide receivers with the Minnesota Vikings. The Vikings acquired Rashad before the 1976 season for a fourth-round draft choice from Seattle, and he became a starter in his fourth game with Minnesota. He has started every game since, highlighting his career there with a club-record 66 catches in 1978.

Rashad was also a record-maker in college at the University of Oregon, where he set 14 school marks, including most receptions for a career (131). He was a running back at Oregon, but became a wide receiver in the pros after the St. Louis Cardinals drafted him on the first round in 1972. He was traded to Buffalo for Dennis Shaw after the 1973 season.

Upon his arrival in Buffalo, Rashad found himself in some pretty good company.

"We had some super people playing offense," he says. "I think we probably had the best offense in football at that time. We had some excellent receivers [J. D. Hill, Bob Chandler, Wallace Francis, and Ray Jarvis along with Rashad], excellent linemen, a really good team offensively. The attitude around the Bills was that O. J. could get 3,000 yards if he wanted that season, because there was just so much talent running the football. It was our feeling that it didn't matter if you knew what we were going to do, we were going to do it anyway. Regardless of what team you were, you were going to have to score 30 points to beat us."

And, of course, the game against Oakland that magic Monday night exemplified the high-powered Buffalo style.

"It was just two good teams with two good offenses going at each other," says Rashad.

Rashad was given the game ball. He still has it. Like the great receiver he is, it's something he would never drop.

CONRAD DOBLER

He is the "Fearsome Foursome" all rolled into one player. He has been called, among other things, "Attila the Hun in football gear," "the meanest man in pro football," and "Dracula."

Does Conrad Dobler take it personally? Of course he does.

"I look at it this way," says the New Orleans Saints' All-Pro player, "I do what I have to do. I enjoy the game. I go out to win. The point of the matter is, if I don't have the 'meanest man' title, then someone else would. And when I get out of the game, someone else will take it over. Anyone of any substance that plays the game, anyone who's been an All-Pro, any good-type football player ends up with some kind of a nickname like that."

So Dobler wears his infamy like badges of honor, which brings us to his most memorable game. Dobler might call it his "Sunday Worst" in keeping with the theme of his football lifestyle. Although he does not consider himself a "bad a——," as he says, he certainly was not on his best behavior this day.

"It's a game," says Dobler, "that will probably haunt me for the rest of my life."

131

For better or worse, and not necessarily in that order, it is the one game that Dobler will always be remembered for.

At the time, Dobler was with the St. Louis Cardinals, a stout team on its way to the National Football League playoffs. They were playing the Miami Dolphins on this particular day in 1977, which happened to be Thanksgiving, and Dobler remembers, "We really had nothing to be thankful for."

The Dolphins crushed the Cardinals 55–14, totaling 503 yards behind a hot-handed Bob Griese, who threw six touchdown passes. Miami's defense held Cardinal rushers to merely 54 yards, picked up two fumbles, and picked off a Jim Hart pass, but that wasn't what Dobler remembered most about the contest.

"There was something like $18,000 to $20,000 in fines handed out," he recalls. "I got fined $1,000 myself. It was certainly one of my most outrageous and embarrassing performances."

Before it was over, Dobler had battled with players, coaches, and referees, thrown his helmet into the stands, and acted generally like the proverbial bull in the china shop.

He left a lot of litter along the way, he remembers.

"It was quite embarrassing, the amount of mail I got after that," he says. "I received hundreds and hundreds of letters. Seventy percent of them were good, but 30 percent were guys calling me a real jerk."

What happened? Well, it wasn't all Dobler's fault, actually.

"It was late in the game and we were taking a real licking," he remembers. "At this particular time, we were supposed to be one of the top offensive lines in the league. We had led the league in the least amount of sacks and everything else. We were supposed to be an aggressive bunch. But that day, it was Miami's offensive line that was doing the job. Bob Griese, their quarterback, really had a hot hand, and he was setting records for pass completions, for touchdowns, and for yardage. He was just eating our defense up.

"Well, the Dolphins' defensive end, A. J. Duhe, was really mouthing off to us. He was saying, 'You guys are a bunch of dogs; we should be playing a high school team,' and stuff like that. Boy, that really burned us up. We had three or four All-Pros on our offensive line, you know?"

At this point, Dobler and his teammates decided to teach "that . . . rookie" a lesson.

"When we got back in the huddle, I looked at Don Deirdorf and Tom Banks and said, 'Hey, listen, we've got to shut that guy up.' What I meant was, once the ball's thrown, and if you're free, if you have nothing else to do, just get him, give him a good shot. On the very next play, one of our tackles cut Duhe off his feet. A. J. was just lying there on his back, and Banks, who was our center, turned around, saw him, and took a five-yard run and speared him in the throat, and rolled over on top of him. So A. J. kind of got up on one knee and was ready to jump on Banks. So I turned around—I was about five yards from him—and just gave Duhe an elbow in the back of his head, and he went down again. There was a bit of a rumble, and the officials broke it up, but they didn't throw me out or anything."

Back in the huddle, Dobler admonished Banks for his overt action.

"I said, let's get him, " Dobler exclaimed, "but I didn't mean to do it illegally."

"I know, I know," Banks shot back, "I just got carried away. The hell with him."

A string of strange coincidences followed that made Dobler look like the "Six Million Dollar Man."

"On the next play, the guy playing over me went down with a knee injury," Dobler recalls. "And on the play after that, the guy playing on top of me went down with a twisted ankle. The next guy suffered a broken rib. So naturally, the Dolphins thought I was doing this on purpose. To be honest with you, I wish I was that bad of an a——. But these things I can honestly say happened by accident. But the point of the matter is, I knew that something was going to hit the fan soon, that they were going to try to get me."

When Dobler went down in his stance for the following play, two Miami linebackers zeroed in on the Cardinal guard.

"One spit on my helmet," Dobler says, referring to Bob Matheson, "and the referee kind of moved over and was watching me. And I said to myself, 'Conrad, if you cause any trouble, they'll throw you out immediately and fine you.' I wasn't making that much money at the time. I knew I had to be cool."

The play started, a draw play, as Dobler remembers. "I had one of these linebackers in front of me and I was screening him off. Well, our back just ran past them, just kept going, but the linebackers were not chasing him . . . these linebackers were still hitting me. So I had to keep my arms up and try to keep them away from me, and finally they just grabbed my face mask and threw me on the ground. Now that I was on the ground, I had to fight."

Fight Dobler did—and so did just about everyone else in the place, too.

"Both benches cleared by this time," remembers Dobler, "and there was another giant fight going on somewhere else on the field. Well, the referees finally broke it up and threw me out of the game. That's what really made me go insane. See, I had played it cool until those linebackers threw me on the ground. Then it was either kick or be kicked. And when the referee pushed me toward the sideline, I kind of reached out and gave him a little nudge. Fortunately, I came to my senses soon enough to catch him before he hit the ground. Now

I had to brush off the referee, because I didn't want to make any more trouble. Hitting a ref is serious stuff. They'll blackball you for that and you'll be out of football forever. I apologized to him real fast."

When Dobler hit the sidelines, Cardinal coach Don Coryell said, "That's okay."

"Well, that was bull," Dobler says. "It wasn't money out of his pocket, it was money out of mine. And I just went crazy then, went wild. I never believed in temporary insanity until that moment. But I do believe, for a minute there I was temporarily insane."

During the course of his rampage, Dobler "knocked a coach down on the sidelines, pulled headphones off his head, threw my helmet into the stands, and hit a couple of players," among other things. "I can't believe how outrageous I was."

Inevitably, bad publicity followed in the Miami press.

"Some of the stories written about me in the Miami papers were outrageously bad. Those idiots were saying this stuff before they saw the films and saw that I really wasn't intentionally injuring those guys; they just came up injured. And I honestly say, when you're winning 55–14 and you lose four starters to injury, that's not my fault, that's a coaching error. They should have never been in there in the first place."

The worst was yet to come for Dobler. He had to visit football commissioner Pete Rozelle in New York for the obligatory wrist-slapping. Dobler was in the city after a Sunday game with the New York Giants and was scheduled to visit the commissioner Monday morning. Dobler recalls with some amusement:

"I went out to a place called the Tittle Tattle Sunday night after the Giants game. I was supposed to see Rozelle eight o'clock the next morning. Well, when I was at this place, Jack Gregory and John Hicks, two New York Giant football players, got into a giant fight, and they kept falling on me and bleeding and I kept pushing them back off me. And the sports pages came out the next day with this story that Conrad Dobler was in the Tittle Tattle fighting. So the next morning, when I walked into Rozelle's office, I was hoping that he hadn't seen the papers yet. I was sitting in his office getting ready to be fined for a fight that I was in the previous week and here I was involved in another mess just four hours before I was supposed to be in his office. It was a tight situation, but if he knew anything about the Tittle Tattle fight, he didn't say anything."

Rozelle and his staff had set up films of the Cardinal-Dolphin game to review Dobler's misbehavior.

"I had never seen films of the game," Dobler recalls, "but I had my defense set up for Rozelle. I was just going to beat him. I was just going to tell him exactly what it was like."

But Dobler's defenses were down after watching his role in the movies.

"We were sitting in these large, studio-type chairs," Dobler recalls, "and before the films were over, my head was so low they didn't know where I was sitting. I couldn't believe how I behaved on the sidelines. And when the films were all over, I just said, well, hell, I don't know what to say; I had no right being out there."

Dobler shakes his head.

"It was Thanksgiving Day, too, and the game was on national television. I'm sure we disturbed a lot of Thanksgiving meals, because a lot of people probably got up from the table to watch that ruckus. It went on for 20 minutes."

Now he grins.

"I can honestly say this: If you're looking at football as an entertainment-type value, that was the only thing exciting that happened in that football game."

Dobler recalls that he left town right after the game for his home in Laramie, Wyoming, to hide away from the rest of the world. Reporters had tried to interview him in the locker room, but he turned them away.

"I didn't really feel like talking to them," says Dobler, usually one of the best interviews in pro football. "I was completely emotionally drained, just plain worn out."

Normally, Dobler recognizes the importance of the reporter-athlete relationship as much as anybody in the game. He considers himself a "pretty good interview. That's why people call me up all the time, because they have a certain amount of inches to fill and they need a certain amount of interesting things to talk about. And my reputation is an interesting subject to write about. Who wants to talk to a defensive tackle who sits there and answers the questions, yes, no, and uh. . . ."

From Dobler, reporters get stories about sleeping in coffins and biting opposing players and jokes. ("I wrote a book, *Everything I Know About Pro Football;* it's empty, a thousand blank pages. . . . I didn't even number them because I didn't want to confuse the reader.")

"I can honestly say that most of the interviews written about me have been pretty much exactly what I've said. But there's a reason for it: I think I've given reporters enough information so that they don't have to read between the lines to figure out what the hell I was talking about."

Dobler's colorful reputation was established in college, when he was a guard and defensive tackle with the University of Wyoming.

"A friend of mine owned a mortuary," Dobler remembers, "and one day we were looking through the coffins. I got in one, just to see how it felt. My friend said, 'How would you like to be stuck in a box like that?' I told him it was pretty damn comfortable. Well, a newspaper guy who overheard us talking about it on a plane ride one time picked it up and wrote a story that I slept in coffins. Things like that snowball, you know."

Dobler's bizarre reputation was enhanced in the pros in a game against the Minnesota Vikings.

"A guy by the name of Doug Sutherland was trying to get to our passer," remembers Dobler, "and he stuck his fingers in my face mask and was dragging me around to try to pull me out of the way. And I just grabbed hold of his wrist near my mouth and bit him. Sutherland never bothered my face mask again that day, and he made the statement that to play Dobler, you needed a string of garlic beads and a stake."

Literally or figuratively, Dobler has been a hard man to pin down most of his life. "I've always liked the action," he says, pointing to innumerable off-the-field interests that include oil drilling rigs in Louisiana, a farm in Iowa, apartments in Wyoming, office buildings, warehouses, a racquetball facility, a radio station, a bar, a bank, and a construction business. The New Orleans Saints' press guide points out that Dobler "owns or has partnerships in 22 businesses."

"It varies, though," says Dobler, "we buy and sell every day."

So Dobler is obviously not your average football-hero-who-lives-next-door type. Nor was he in college, where he was not only All–Western Athletic Conference as a player but also an all-academic selection. He holds a degree in political science, not basket weaving, by the way.

What new fields are there for him to conquer?

"A windmill," says Dobler.

That needs some further explanation, of course.

"My folks had a windmill in our yard when I was a kid," he says. "That windmill stood there and had a ladder that went to the top of it, and I climbed it a little bit higher every year. But, you know, I always chickened out before I got to the very top. Eventually, I had it in mind that I was going to touch the top of that son of a gun, but they sold it when I went away to college. It made me angry that I had the opportunity for ten years to touch the top of that thing and now it's gone. I feel like I didn't follow through on a commitment of my life. It sounds funny, I guess, but that darned windmill has been sort of a motivational force for me all these years. I think about it all the time. One of these days, I'm going to find one out in the pasture and climb it all the way to the top."

For a man who has already climbed mountains, a little windmill shouldn't be so tough.

RON JAWORSKI

After 13 straight losses in Dallas, the Philadelphia Eagles were starting to feel unlucky.

And here they were, in a hole again in 1979, after a quick-strike touchdown by the Cowboys after only 61 seconds of the game.

"At that point," remembers Philadelphia quarterback Ron Jaworski, "we felt, oh boy, here we go, it's going to be another one of those long days."

But just when the Eagles seemed headed in the wrong direction, Jaworski got them turned around. And before you could say, "Roger Staubach," Philadelphia's whipping boys were on their way to a 31–21 National Football League victory over their longtime tormentors.

So Jaworski has no doubt about his most memorable game in football.

"It was a game that is very memorable now and probably will become more memorable five or ten years from now," says Jaworski. "In our minds, Dallas is number one, the team that we have to shoot for every year to beat and be a contender in our division. We hadn't won a game in Dallas in 13 years, and ever since the opening of training camp we were pointing toward Dallas. On the first day of training camp, I remember, coach (Dick)

Vermeil made one of our goals this season to beat the Dallas Cowboys at least once. So it was the kind of game that not only had the buildup of one week, but four months."

Putting added pressure on the Eagles was the fact that this was a "must" victory for them at this particular time of the season. They had lost three straight games and Jaworski admits, "Things were looking pretty bleak for us. We were still in contention for the [division] title, but we weren't playing well."

The contest as well was being played on the weekly Monday night television broadcast, a circumstance that really put on the pressure.

In the week-long practice before the game, Jaworski could feel the tension building up among the Eagle players. "When you play a good team like that, there's always a bit of tension involved, and I noticed that we were a bit uptight prior to that game," he says. "It's very difficult to be optimistic when you haven't won in 13 years in a place and you're playing a team with as many skilled players as they have. We knew it would take a fine effort to beat them."

The Cowboys started out as if they would run (or actually throw) the Eagles right out of Texas Stadium, as Staubach hurled a 48-yard touchdown pass to Tony Hill on the third play of the game. With barely a minute gone, the Eagles were trailing 7–0, and Jaworski, along with the other Philadelphia players, was feeling a little sick.

"When a team brings it down the field that quickly, you know, you just get the feeling it's going to be that kind of day. But fortunately, our offense got going and our defense really tightened up and we played good defense the rest of the game. Offensively, I'd say we had a pretty good day, too. When you score 31 points against Dallas, that's a great day. Normally, you have a tough time scoring ten points against those guys."

The Eagles, as all good teams do, took advantage of

their opponent's mistakes to change the flow of momentum.

"The real turning point was when we had attempted a long field goal and missed, but the Cowboys were offside on the play," Jaworski recalls. "So now, instead of it being fourth-and-six, it became fourth-and-one, and coach Vermeil decided to go for it. It was on their 30-yard line, or somewhere around there, and we called a play-action fake and I completed a touchdown pass to Harold Carmichael. That tied the score at 7–7 and kind of got our motors running and gave us the opportunity to get back into the ballgame.

"And then again, we had a good drive going at the start of the third quarter, and I hit Harold in the end zone on a corner route, which, you know, boosted our lead at that time [to 24–7]. So they were two big plays, two big passing plays, that I felt I made a contribution to the victory."

As the final score indicates, of course, there was a lot more to the game than that—even though Jaworski's second touchdown pass, of 13 yards, actually provided the Eagles with their winning points. For instance: Tony Franklin kicked a 59-yard field goal for the Eagles, second longest in NFL history; Jaworski sprained his wrist and had to sit out a while; and the Cowboys made things interesting at the end with two quick touchdown passes from none other than the redoubtable Staubach.

In short, said Jaworski, "It was a game that had all the excitement and the thrills of a Super Bowl. It was a very emotional high for the whole three-hour period; there were no lulls, it was just a real dogfight. It was such an emotional and physical game that everybody was just drained afterwards. I remember on the flight back home, everybody was too tired to celebrate. The guys grabbed a sandwich and a drink, and I noticed that more than half of our players were sleeping on the plane."

Jaworski had to be wide awake, though, thinking

about what he had accomplished in his short career with the Eagles. One of the NFL's bright young quarterbacks, Jaworski immediately took charge of the no. 1 job in Philadelphia upon his arrival in 1977. Previously, the Youngstown State graduate had been a second-round draft choice of the Los Angeles Rams in 1973, but had a generally undistinguished career as a backup quarterback there for three seasons. He was acquired by Philadelphia for tight end Charles Young on March 9, 1977, and in his second full season as a starter, in 1978, he led the Eagles to the playoffs.

Instrumental in Jaworski's development has been the great faith placed in him by Philadelphia coach Dick Vermeil.

"It's amazing what confidence will do for a quarterback," says Jaworski. "When I was in Los Angeles, the feeling was that if you made a mistake, they would put someone else in. But in Philadelphia, I can take a chance. Maybe my pass will be picked off, but I don't have to worry about coming to the sidelines and having a coach chew me out or seeing someone else warming up. I can make a mistake and profit by it rather than have it hurt me."

Since coming to Philadelphia and working with Vermeil, a ball control-style coach, Jaworski has changed his operational procedures considerably.

"I used to be a riverboat-gambler type of quarterback," he says. "I was always looking for the big play. Sometimes I would try to force the play. Now I try to be more efficient, take what the defense gives me instead of trying to force the issue. Establishing a winning game plan, a winning program, there has to be a proper correlation between running and passing. Dick has toned me down and given me a real understanding of what it takes to win. I believe that his thinking is now mine. I'm convinced now that's the way to win in this league."

The big victory over Dallas in 1979 triggered the

Eagles toward their second straight playoff berth. Once they got started in this game, they pretty much accomplished what they had set out to do.

"Prior to the game," says Jaworski, "we felt the key was getting good yards on first down. First down was going to be our most important down. Usually it always is, but against the Cowboys it's even more so because they have such a great secondary package that they kill you in third-and-long situations. But more than that, they have those great rush people . . . you know, Harvey Martin, Randy White, and Larry Cole. They can really come after you, so you want to stay out of those situations. We were very fortunate to be successful on first downs for the most part and were able to keep those big horses off me."

After his 32-yard TD strike to Carmichael tied the game, Jaworski could see the Eagles "loosening up and getting down to what they should be getting down to: scoring points and shutting down people defensively."

Which is exactly what they did for a while, even though Jaworski couldn't personally enjoy all of it. Jaworski had injured his wrist on a sack by Martin and was being x-rayed when backup quarterback John Walton fired a 29-yard scoring pass to Charles Smith that gave the Eagles a 14–7 lead with 1:03 remaining in the first half. The Philadelphia touchdown was set up by Frank LeMaster's recovery of Steve Wilson's fumble at the Dallas 29.

The Philadelphia defense again was instrumental in setting up another score for the Eagles, as safety Randy Logan intercepted a pass by Danny White, who was substituting for the injured Staubach, at the Dallas 42. The Cowboys held, but with 27 seconds left in the half Franklin kicked his gigantic 59-yard field goal, a club record and only four yards short of Tom Dempsey's NFL record of 63 yards.

"Tony told me he could make it," said a stunned Vermeil, "so I told him, okay, so go do it."

The Cowboys were equally shocked.

"When he kicked that field goal right before the half, it just took something out of us," said Dallas coach Tom Landry. "It was just a spectacular kick . . . we didn't think he could kick it that far, or we would have taken an offsides penalty [against Philadelphia] on the play before. We couldn't believe it."

So in 46 seconds the Eagles had scored ten points, and they took a 17–7 lead into the dressing room at halftime. But still they weren't completely satisfied.

"Parts of our halftime conversation dealt with our running game," Jaworski remembers. "It was just that we weren't running the ball in the first half as well as we were capable of doing. Basically, we're a ball-control team and we like to chew up the clock and get a lot of yards on the ground, and I think in the first half we had something like ten yards rushing. So we came out in the second half and rushed for some 160 yards. We kind of turned our running game around in the second half; we ball-controlled them, and you know, when Roger Staubach doesn't have the ball, it's pretty hard for the Dallas Cowboys to score."

By the time the third quarter started, Jaworski's wrist wasn't bothering him enough to keep him from playing. He picked up where he left off, directing the Eagles on a 57-yard, nine-play touchdown drive that culminated with his 13-yard scoring pass to Carmichael with 6:38 to play in the third period. That gave the Eagles a 24–7 lead and a cushion sufficient to withstand two touchdown passes by Staubach in the game's last six minutes.

After Dallas had cut the Eagles' lead to 24–21 on Staubach's five-yard TD pass to Billy Joe DuPree with 1:17 left, the Cowboys attempted an onside kick. But the ploy failed and the Eagles started running out the clock. With a minute to go and the Eagles facing a third-and-two situation, Wilbert Montgomery raced 37 yards around left end for Philadelphia's final touchdown.

The victory meant so much to the Eagles, one writer pointed out, that the Philadelphia locker room afterward "was like a college dressing room with some players turning on local writers, shouting: 'Get on the bandwagon.' Vermeil celebrated his first victory in six tries over the Cowboys with hugs and backslaps with his players."

"You know, from a statistical standpoint, it wasn't even near what my best day had been," says Jaworski, who completed only 12 of 29 passes for 145 yards. "But from a team standpoint and from the emotion involved in the game, it was a game that obviously will be one I'll never forget. Everything seemed to be against us. It was in a place where we hadn't won for 13 years, and we hadn't been playing good ball of late. But it was the type of game that we had pointed for for a long time. And fortunately, we got the job done. That victory gave us a lot of confidence . . . a feeling that if we can beat Dallas at home, we can beat them anywhere, and we can beat any team anywhere."

About The Author

Ken Rappoport is a veteran writer who has covered every major sport for The Associated Press. He has ten books to his credit, including two previous Tempo titles, *Great College Football Rivalries* and *Diamonds in the Rough*. In addition, he has contributed to four other books and several national magazines. He resides in New Jersey with his wife, Bernice, his three children, Felicia, Sharon, and Larry, and his mother and father.